Forget me not

nicole bea

ISBN: 978-1-68046-882-3

Fire & Ice Young Adult Books
An Imprint of Melange Books, LLC
White Bear Lake, MN 55110
www.fireandiceya.com

Published in the United States of America.

Cover Design by Caroline Andrus

ONE

~ PAISLEY ~

It's seven o'clock in the morning, and I'm standing on the edge of the roof, looking across the street at Mitchell's house. The window to his room is easy to spot, not from the location but because the daybreak hits his window at exactly the right position that it refracts the light and shines into my eyes. I'm temporarily blinded—the spotty black bits in my line of vision soon disappearing so that the brick-front house comes back into view again. The curtains in his room are still drawn, but the checkered pattern is clear through the glass.

There's something beautiful and nostalgic about the way the sunrise looks from the top of my house as the orange and yellow flames lick away at the cotton candy of the sky. The new day drops rays of lemony shade on the valley below Hollyberry Subdivision, twinkling crystals on the Sawyer River in its infinite blue. It's a peaceful moment, those seconds where the crows quiet and allows for the songbirds to call their melody of the morning. To be fair, I can use all the peaceful mornings I can get—the ones I have left are numbered now.

I'll never forget the exact moment the doctor told my family there was nothing else he could do for me because the tumors had spread to my brain. The room had cheerful blue walls, while I was taped up and attached to machines that whirred next to me and counted a number of things from my heart rate to my medication levels. The words dripped over me like a leaking faucet—not fast enough to make you wet but at enough of a consistency to make you aware of a problem. I was waterproof at that moment, the trickles of terminology sliding off my skin and only being picked up my mother—in person—and my father, on the phone from his oil rig out in the middle of the ocean.

When Doctor Aker spoke those words, the ones meant to indicate that I wasn't going to be around much longer, my mother cried her eyes out in the hospital room while a red splotchiness spread on her cheeks in the shape of butterfly wings. Hugging my numb body tight, she nearly pulled out the intravenous line to my arm, her sobs echoing along the mossy grey accent walls. Dad was probably crying too, although the last time I remember him doing such a thing was when Auntie Ella died when I was seven. She was in an unfortunate winter car accident where someone without snow tires slid into the back of her Ford F-150, smashing it right off a residential bridge into highway traffic below.

I'm glad that's not the way I'm going to go, staring face down at the terrified expressions of innocent people milliseconds before my vehicle crushes them to death. Though I guess there are some similarities in the circumstances, Auntie Ella's seems a lot more dramatic. My way of going out is going to be like so many others— slow and boring, with nothing to make the end of my life any more special than the others.

While the sun rose on my diagnosis, and the songbirds tweeted out a symphony like the ones easily heard from the rooftop today, Doctor Aker sat on the edge of the empty bed beside me, my double occupancy room cleared of anyone who could overhear my prognosis. His hands, red and wrought, folded on his lap in thoughtful contemplation as he apologized for something he could never have changed. I'm sure he had given the speech about a half a million times before, but that didn't seem to help make him any less nervous in presenting the circumstance. A thought rolled over in my mind—if it ever got any easier telling patients they're going to die. Part of me wanted to ask him, but it seemed like an out of place question seeing as I was supposed to be the one having all the feelings, not him.

Once Mom had her initial reaction, my own blank mind not letting me feel anything, Doctor Aker advised us that my medical team was going to send me home. For a moment the statement was freeing—I'd finally get out of this bed—then the truth of the matter hit, cold and hard and mortal. After two years of being in and out of Birch Valley Regional Hospital, I was being released to die a quiet death in the little pre-war house I had grown up in. The way Doctor Aker described it was as peaceful as this morning, lying in my own bed on my own terms, slipping away in my sleep as if I'm some little old lady who's had the fortune of existing an entire lifetime. Instead, I soon realized, I'm just getting screwed out of everything I'm supposed to have the opportunity to experience.

And so, now I have a plan.

Every once and awhile throughout the de-hospitalization process, an idea would pop into my head of something I was bound to miss—prom, graduation, falling in love, the legal drinking age, getting married—and I'd scribble it down in my little teal journal. The book was a gift from Dad when I first got sick, a gentle thought to write down my last hopes and wishes. Now the pages are wrinkled with ideas, doodles, and shower-thoughts where I yell at God and feel sorry for myself before putting on my strong façade and custom black mastectomy bra, so I almost feel normal.

I don't have the bra on right now. The façade doesn't come onto the rooftop with me. I can be my angry self here.

There's a little wisp of violet cloud that gets sucked into the tree line as my phone buzzes on the shingles. The sound knocks me out of my daydream if you could call it that, reminding me that I'm still very much alive.

Mitchell: *Morning, Songbird.*

Mitchell's been calling me that since the fifth grade when I tried out for the city choir. The whole situation was so embarrassing; I've never tried to relay the details to anyone else for fear of being constantly bombarded with reminders about my ridiculousness. I don't know why Mitchell ended up knowing about it; he knows a lot more about me than most people do, from secrets to hopes and dreams, and everything is written in that little teal journal. Well, just about everything.

Paisley: *Morning. Happy Tuesday.*

Mitchell: *You know, I see you sitting on the roof from my place.*

Paisley: *Don't ruin the allure of the position, Mitchell.*

Mitchell: *Hey now, you know that's a benefit and not a deterrent.*

Mitchell texts faster than I can think up a witty response, and there's no doubt in my mind he's sitting over there in his bed waiting for a message back. As I consider it, there's a little wiggling feeling in the pit of my stomach. He's probably not wearing a shirt. Or maybe not even pants.

Flipping the phone over abruptly, face down and away from the light, I place it back on the scratchy black rooftop. By the time our exchange ends, there's already a little peek of the sun coming over the valley, and I'm reminded with a silent internal alarm that I need to get ready for school. Normally, someone in my position would be plagued with daily medications, visits from medical professionals, poked with needles and prodded with instruments. A week ago yesterday, I was sent back home with a boatload of drugs, the number of a personal healthcare nurse, and all of Doctor Aker's well-wishes.

Mom's never called the number. I told her not to bother. The medication is negligible depending on the day. I don't want to spend my last few weeks or months or whatever I have left feeling like garbage, and that's all the medication seems to do is make me feel worse than I already do.

Like a lightbulb, a perfect text pops into my head, and I grab my phone to type it out. There's something about my relationship with Mitchell that I can't quite put my finger on. It might be the fact that I might be in love with him but maybe that's just something that happens between girls and guys as they get older. Maybe everything has a way of changing.

Paisley: *The only benefit is knowing that you're over there thinking of me when you first wake up. That says something.*

Mitchell: *Yeah, it says that you live across the street and are standing on the roof in short shorts. Way to get a guy's attention.*

There's a knock on my bedroom door, and I scramble through the window frame with my phone in hand, interrupting the sleep of my golden lab, Ivy. Mom hates it when I sit out there. She's convinced I'm going to fall off the roof and die.

Joke's on her.

"Paisley, there's some magazines here with your name on them that came in with the bills yesterday. They look like travel catalogs?" The sound of mail being flipped through casually trickles under the door.

I haul myself off the wooden window sill and toss the phone on my quilt as I cross the room. Ivy's eyes follow the trajectory of the device, and she lets out a single bark as it hits the bed. Padding my bare feet over the rug and then the laminate floor, I open my door to a puff of chilly air. Mom's hands are sorting through the envelopes, and she flips the glossy magazines over to face me.

"Yeah, I went online and requested some. Figure I can at least pretend I'm going to get to do some things." The red sand beaches of Partridge Island catch my eye, and I flip a pamphlet over and read the description of Keystone Beach on the back.

"Paisley, don't be so morbid. You've been doing better than the doctor expected." My mother likes to remind me of this fact on a semi-regular basis as if I'm going to forget.

I learned long ago that it's important to be thankful for every day because at any time you might get notice that you're going to die. The unlucky people get no notice at all. I'm pretty sure I'd rather know than not know.

"Do you think I'll make it to prom?"

Mom drops the rest of the mail on the hallway table, not accepting my dramatic tone for anything other than what it is—an over-reaction.

"Honey, it's only three days away. Unless you fall off that roof, I'm sure it's going to be no big deal." Mom winks at me, and because of this, it's clear that I've left the window gaping open, giving myself away. My face turns a bright pink, judging by the prickles of heat crawling up the back of my neck and over my face. "You need to keep a positive attitude. Doctor Aker said that's important."

"Yeah." I drop the catalogs on my dresser, the surface piled high with clothes. A couple of magazines wobble precariously on the edge of a bundle of jeans, then slips off and slides to the floor with a little flop. As I reach down to grab them, there's a pain behind my left eye that starts as a sensation of being stabbed and then begins to throb so painfully I am forced to feel for the door frame before the world turns entirely fuzzy all around the edges. Sliding my back against the wall and reaching out for Mom's hand to guide me, I drop the catalogs back to the floor with tiny slaps.

"Another one?" The scent of Mom's shampoo reigns over everything else, the scent of coconuts and papayas ramming me in the face with pain. "Do you want me to call Doctor Aker?"

I shake my head, the movement making me feel as if I'm underwater.

"I'm fine, just dying. All part of the process."

The quiet hum of the house serves as background noise while Mom and I wait for the pain to subside. She sits across from me against the hallway wall, her lithe runner's frame bunched up with knees to the chest and one hand holding my own. It starts to wane in the same way it always does, but I don't know if it takes ten seconds, ten minutes, or ten hours. There's something infinite about hurt.

"You know you don't have to go to school, Ley." Mom pushes her shoulders against the tanned hide color of the hallway and uses her free hand to scratch under her chignon.

"But it's almost over."

To be fair, so is everything.

I don't say that out loud though, because it would only depress my mother. My father and I are the ones with the dark and dry sense of humor.

"Why don't you text Georgia and Taryn and see if they want to do a little bit of shopping. Maybe you can find a dress this afternoon after school. I'll give you my card before you go." Mom refers to two members of my five-person friend group—together since the days of preschool and partners in crime ever since.

"Great, I'll text them both once my vision comes back. If I don't make it to prom, you can always bury me in it," I say with a groan.

Mom slaps my leg with an unopened white envelope.

"At least you still have your sense of humor, Paisley. Guess you're not quite ready to go yet."

I might smile and can't tell because everything is upside down and painful. It's unclear to me whether or not my facial muscles actually work, or if I'm actually making a strange expression that barely comes across as a grin.

"On second thought," I mumble with my eyes closed, my head heavy and sore, "maybe I will stay home today."

There's a thump, and a staccato set of clicks as Ivy trots along the floor to place herself down next to me, her head in my lap. The shuffling of Mom reaching over to pat the dog before she lets go of my hand and stands up.

"Ivy, you stay here with Paisley until she's ready to crawl back to bed. You're a good girl."

I close my eyes, place my hand on Ivy's head, and wish to whatever God is up there to please just give me this one last summer to get everything marked off my bucket list. Then whoever takes people off the earth can have me. Not one second sooner.

TWO

~ PAISLEY ~

Sleeping is bliss.

Even before I got sick, I could spend entire days in bed, wrapping myself in the smell of lavender detergent and clean linen. I'd pick up a book, fix myself under particularly arranged covers, and read next to the dog until the sky drew weary of shining. The words would transport me outside, to other worlds, to places I'd only read about. Now, the bed is almost a prison, a place where I stay out of force rather than desire.

I blink a couple of times at the sunlight streaming through the curtains, trying to evaluate the way my head feels and see if the better part of my eyesight has returned. There's a bit of a haze around the edges—the doctor called it an aura, once—but the hammering pain has subsided into an occasional simulated heartbeat in my skull. It's liveable.

The crisp crinkle of a bed sheet tells me Ivy's departed for her water bowl, and I use the opportunity to roll over and call Georgia about dress shopping. A selfie of her swimming in Sawyer River pops up on my screen as I select her contact, the perfect image to represent her personality: wild and free. Especially since the end of winter term.

Dean Kehoe and Georgia have been hiding the fact that they're sleeping together for a bare minimum of a couple of months, if not longer. The two of them think that the rest of us don't know, but we do. I've always had an inkling, thanks to a slip of the tongue from Georgia one night. She doesn't think Dean and her will ever be a thing—they've known each other too long—and decided last week just to keep her mouth shut and ride the thing out until she goes away to university in Ontario in September. Dean, being a man, is all right with this arrangement. I don't know how it makes me feel, the idea of my friends using one another for a more adult type of companionship.

I practically picture Georgia flicking her ponytail behind her shoulder as she picks up the phone.

"Hi, Ley."

"Hey, what's going on?" My voice sounds weak in comparison, probably giving away to Georgia that I've had another one of my episodes. She doesn't bother mentioning the inflection of my voice anymore, half because she already knows what it means, and the other half because it doesn't matter anyway.

"Just sitting around, texting Dean to see what's going on for the weekend and reminding him to pick me up a white corsage. Resisting the urge to put on my prom dress now and wear it until the dance. What are you doing?"

I prop the phone up with my shoulder and rub at my scalp, sad little tufts of hair grazing on the surface.

"Well, speaking of prom, it looks like I'm going to be able to make it. If I don't croak in the next three days."

Georgia seems not to be able to help herself; she lets out a little squeal that pierces the phone line.

"Yes! That makes me so happy! Have you found a dress? What about a date? If you want to come over early, I can do your hair."

I appreciate the enthusiasm, but it feels like a little bit much. The idea of getting my hair done all fancy for the big dance was something I had looked forward to since the beginning of high school. I used to have thick, chestnut locks the color of a chocolate lab. Now, thanks to all the rounds of chemotherapy and radiation and medication, I don't have any left; just dwindling little springs, like grass trying to grow through sand.

"Slow your roll, G. I have no dress, no date, and no hair. You can only mitigate so many of those." Ivy hops back up on the bed and turns around in at least three circles before lying down.

"Right. Well, let's work one at a time then?"

"That's what I was thinking—you and Taryn could help me look for something?"

"Of course, I have literally nothing else to do. Want me to come to pick you up in twenty? I'll holler at Taryn out the window and see if she's around. Knock something off that bucket list of yours—wear a red dress to prom."

Taryn and Georgia are neighbors, their bedroom windows facing one another.

"What, the red dress thing? I dunno about that, G. Maybe I'll look for something a little more subdued. I don't need a bunch of people with an excuse to stare at me." I begin to feel a lot more nervous than I appear. Red's so bright. I don't really want anyone looking at me. They already stare at me enough. And whisper. Always so many whispers like they've never seen anyone with cancer before.

"Honey, people are so self-centered they'll barely notice anyone besides themselves. You do you. We'll find you a red dress."

I'm not convinced, but Georgia has this way about her that almost makes it sound like everything's going to be all right.

"Okay," I reply with some hesitation, not entirely sold on the idea of actually being able to go to prom. There's still one issue. "Just… will it be weird if I don't have a date? I don't want to waste my time if it will be weird."

In the background, I hear her slide her window open, the wood frame crunching on the old house.

"Please. Ask Mitchell. He's still petrified of girls, so I doubt he's asked anyone."

"Mitchell has abs now," I remind her, remembering the day he showed them off in a quiet corner of the school stairwell. "I don't think he's allowed to be scared for much longer."

Georgia snorts into my ear, and Taryn's voice warbles through the speaker of the phone even though I can't make out the words. Clearly, she's talking to Georgia, who is doing a well enough job at holding two conversations at the same time.

"Fine." I sigh, not really meaning to agree. "I'll text Mitchell and see if he might actually still be free to go."

"There's my girl. I'll pick you up in fifteen."

She hangs up without another word and I assume this is my cue to get myself ready and prepare my body for public viewing. I've been rolling around in bed all day, so I hop into the shower, just a quick, hot rinse to get the smell of dog and bed sheets off my body. It takes me all of two minutes, leaving thirteen extra to spare, in which I stand in front of the full-length mirror in the bathroom and wonder if I'll ever look like a regular human again. Women are supposed to be curvy and voluptuous; I'm just flat all over. I used to love reading fashion magazines before I got sick, but now I find they only remind me that I'm disfigured and don't fit properly into my clothes anymore.

Georgia pulls into my driveway a half hour later (because let's face it, she's always late for everything), the metallic paint of her black sedan making tiny prisms as it reflects the bright outdoor light. I'm perched on the front step in my favorite pair of jeans, picking away at a hole in the knee and letting the late-day sun warm my face as it travels across the expansive lawn of my house.

Georgia, Taryn, and I used to ride our stick horses on this lawn, eating peanut butter and jam sandwiches while we'd pretend we were touring the Australian outback. Now the space is a healthy green and free from our trampling footsteps, while my ride-on pony is up in the attic somewhere, rotting away with dust and age and time. Sometimes I miss those days. The days before I knew that something was wrong with me.

Tugging open the back door, I toss in my canvas bag and slide my way across the upholstery to sit in the middle seat of the bench.

"Hey!" I greet the two of them simultaneously and fasten my seat belt.

"Hey to you. Did you text Mitchell? We're working on a tight timeline."

Of course, Georgia is right down to business.

"Not exactly," I hesitate saying as she backs her way out of the drive. This affords her the opportunity to glare at me as if I were a naughty child. "Okay, no. I didn't. Prom isn't exactly Mitchell's cup of tea, you know."

The car shifts noisily into gear.

"Just do it, Ley. You know Georgia won't stop until you do." Taryn turns in her seat and gives me a knowing look. We've all been part of Georgia's schemes before, and sometimes it's just easier to go with them, rather than against them.

I pull my phone from the canvas bag, shuffling around my wallet and old, discarded receipts.

Paisley: *Hey, question for you. Looks like I'm going to make it to prom. G said you might not have a date?*

"There. I sent him a message," I announce. "Are you happy now?"

"Very." Georgia's hands go over one another to turn the corner at the end of Main Street. Taryn uses the opportunity to commandeer Georgia's cell phone and shuffle through to a song I don't recognize. It has a thick bass line and some electronic melody; a club tune with a name that's probably unrelated to anything, like Jackpot or Carpet-Blaster.

I place my phone on the seat next to me, digging around in my bag for a specific crumpled up piece of pale yellow paper. It's a little bit wrinkled, folded over and over on top of itself, my wide writing spread across the thin black lines. The words are my own—all ten of the things I wrote on my bucket list when I texted them to the other four members of my group from the stark, white hospital room. I made copies and ripped them from my teal notebook and handed one to Taryn, Georgia, Dean, and Mitchell on their various visits to see me.

Have the perfect summer.

Get drunk for the first time.

Fall in love.

My heart and my head flicker to Mitchell, barely before I even realize that they both do it. I've been harboring something for him for the better part of senior year, a little blue flame that I keep deep in my chest because the idea of letting him know there's even a minutia of attraction seems absolutely unfair.

I'm dying for Christ's sake.

I fold the paper up again, a terrible form of origami.

I will not fall in love with Mitchell, and Mitchell will not fall in love with me.

The paper tumbles back into my bag, balled up in the corner against an ink-dead pen and a packet of bubble gum. It looks like a tiny carnation, ragged petals of ivory against the espresso interior of the bag—the kind of flower that my father had pinned to his lapel when we attended our cousin Emily's wedding last year.

Taryn changes the song again, a rock hit slamming into my ears and scattering my memories.

We get halfway to the mall before Mitchell answers my message, probably occupied with binge-reading linking Wikipedia articles or talking to his brother Nolan in Alberta.

Mitchell: *True—wasn't planning on going. But if it's your last wish and all I'll make an appearance.*

Paisley: *Funny. Was hoping maybe you'd be my date. Friend date. You know.*

Mitchell: *Only if you buy a red dress. Seems like that's the only color tie I own, just in case you were worried about matching.*

His laugh sounds in my head even though he isn't in the immediate vicinity. I've been listening to it for thirteen years and count-ing, and there's a little piece of my head that holds essential personal characteristics, then another part of my head that contains every detail about Mitchell that I could ever possibly want to remember.

Paisley: *I'm in the car with G and T right now. I'll be sure to consider that. I don't think they're going to let me forget that it was on my bucket list.*

Mitchell: *What's your favorite kind of flower?*

He spells flower wrong about six times before he actually gets the sentence out, damn autocorrect.

Paisley: *Oh please. Don't do that. Don't do the flower thing. We're friends.*

Every time I say that we're friends it pushes that pebble in my organs a little bit deeper. As if I don't already know that we're friends. As if I don't know that I'm dying, and we aren't going to be able to be friends all that much longer. As if the thought of it all doesn't totally consume me, distracting me from the cancer and the rounds of chemotherapy and radiation.

THREE

~ MITCHELL ~

Prom isn't exactly my cup of jack and coke, but when Paisley texts to ask me to go, it's clear I have to suck it up.

It's not that I don't want to attend exactly—I appreciate that prom for what it is—it's more about the fact I don't particularly like being the new object of attraction to the popular girls just because I finally started to grow up. My dad always says that muscles don't make a man, but he also used to be a bodybuilder, so I'm not sure exactly what message I'm supposed to take from the advice. Plus, Rachel and Karen and the other girls seem to think otherwise, and it's uncomfortable getting groped like a piece of meat.

I rise from my computer chair where I've been binge-reading linking Wikipedia articles for the last hour and a half, gazing into my closet for the possibility of something to wear. Near the back, behind my pile of winter cardigans, is a charcoal grey suit that used to belong to my older brother Nolan, who left it here before he moved off to Alberta. I have no idea what a normal person would wear to prom, but I'm a little late now in trying to order in a tux, so I suppose Nolan's hand-me-down will have to do in a pinch. Thankfully, something somewhere in my brain remembers that Paisley wanted a red dress, and I manage to locate a crimson silk tie in a tangle underneath a pair of boxed up, black dress shoes.

Guess that's it then, I'm going to prom, and it took me all of twenty seconds to plan my outfit. Meanwhile Paisley's going to be out with the girls for hours trying to scrounge up something she feels half decent in. Girls always get the short end of the stick with these kinds of things. I plop into my computer chair and roll backward until I hit the wall with a hollow thud.

Paisley and I have been in this weird place since I started to get noticed. It's almost as if she's jealous I'm getting attention from outside of our usual friend group, but then again if she's started to develop feelings toward me that require more than friendship, she's never divulging it. I've never thought about her in that way, the way that's attraction versus a platonic relationship, but when I start to there's a little bubble that forms down in my stomach, and I have to kick it away.

I can't help the smile that cracks across my face. For someone with a limited timeline, it's admirable that Paisley still has the energy to get out and try to enjoy the rest of her life. If I knew I was going to die, I don't know if I could put all my most reasonable hopes and dreams into a bulleted list. There are so many places to go and things to experience it seems harrowing to know Paisley's going to miss out on some of the best ones based purely on circumstance.

Life isn't fair.

I put my phone face-down on my desk and pull a piece of paper from the top drawer, pushing a stack of watercolor paints from the top. The words aren't my own, however. They belong to Paisley— all ten of the things she wrote on her bucket list when she texted them to the four of us from her hospital room. Following the text we all got copies of the note in her bubbly handwriting; a little treasure map of Paisley to have and to hold. Something about me feels responsible for remembering them as if in my own way I could ever make any of them happen. Facilitating prom is about as far as I expect to get, and maybe that's good enough for her, but it doesn't comfort me at all.

I click my laptop shut and flatten the page on the cover, rubbing my thumb into my left eye to keep the tears back.

Learn to speak French.

Number one on the list. I certainly hope that the items are in no particular order of importance because I've learned how to say a total of two words in the language—*pomme de terre* and *pamplemousse*. I don't think that's really what she's referring to, and my core French classes didn't manage to stick from junior high all the way through to now. To help Paisley, I'd have to learn to speak French first, and I don't think anyone has time for that.

Graduate.

Number six. Nothing I do or don't do will make this one happen, although Paisley has decent grades and definitely was on the grad list posted outside the principal's office. Other than the academic requirements that she's more than met, I assume the big man upstairs will have control of whether or not she's well enough to attend. It's looking like yes.

Fall in love.

Number eight. A dainty thing that can't be rushed and shouldn't be faked; every time I read the three words that little air bubble in my stomach comes up again. It sits like a pebble inside of my heart, cutting off blood flow to all the aware parts of my body and diverting it elsewhere. I don't want to think about Paisley in that way, but with the image of the red dress in my head and the sound of her laugh in my ears, I don't seem to be able to help myself. It's a peculiar thing.

I scratch one-handed at the five o'clock shadow creeping over my face, the prickly hairs tickling my fingertips, as I try to think of something else to say to Paisley just to keep her texting throughout her dress shopping process.

Nolan is the one who is good with girls, always knowing what to wear and what to say and who to say it to in order to get the best attention from whatever person interests him at the time. If he wasn't in Alberta, maybe I could ask him about this whole situation with Paisley, but I don't know that he'd be all that sympathetic to not wanting to get in bed with a girl who is dying with the last wish of falling in love.

I can't be that guy.

More time must go past than I am able to keep track of because there's another beep on my phone with a photo message from Paisley.

Paisley: *I found a dress. You're officially roped into going to prom.*

I click on the photo to load it, the wireless internet doing its regular regime of being shitty in my bedroom. My brain aches as the loading circle takes its own sweet time, torturing me into waiting to see Paisley in whatever number she's found at the last possible second.

Then it's done.

Paisley's sent me a selfie in a mall dressing room mirror, a flaming red dress with a sequin and sparkly top that hits the floor and splays like a gentle waterfall. It falls over her body in a size that must be at least two smaller than she was previously, the thinness of her waist contrasted by the rippled fabric. The black bob wig combined with the edgy color is startling and stunning.

But she's still sick, I tell myself.

Paisley: *Do you think it will be alright? Does it match your tie?*

Mitchell: *I like it, Songbird. Don't wear heels or you'll be taller than me.*

My heart is trying to smash through my ribcage.

Damn it, Mitchell. Get a grip.

Paisley: *You're going to have to give up that name eventually, you know.*

Mitchell: *Make me.*

I add a little winking face at the end, just for good measure.

Georgia calls me later, all in a hurry, and I can tell she's had an idea by the way she's already started talking before I've picked up. She's a spitfire when it comes to managing her emotions in our regular, friend life, and Dean says that fiery attitude isn't at all dampened when it comes to handling her in bed. He's described dating Georgia as a little bit sinful and a little like living in hell, but I promised him I'd never say anything to her because all of this is happening under cover of darkness. Some days are harder than others to pretend like I don't know they're hooking up.

Something about spending the night out with Paisley and Taryn has torn Georgia up more than usual, leaving her distracted by anything and everything. As much as I've tried, I can't imagine how she feels. On top of that, it has also become increasingly difficult to decipher how Dean feels, seeing as he is obviously and ardently in love with the girl. He really should just tell her and see where it goes.

But who am I to judge? I'm doing this awkward act of pining after a girl that I sat next to in kindergarten and once fed an unwrapped yellow crayon telling her it was a noodle.

Life has a funny way of going.

"Mitchell? Are you even listening to me?"

I haven't been listening, so I start up a comment of my own.

"So Paisley's going to make it to prom, eh? I'm glad for her. Get one thing off that bucket list of hers. But what's the plan for the rest of it?"

Georgia doesn't respond for a minute, as if it takes her last remaining bit of energy to come up with a suitable answer and not yell at me for my distraction.

"I don't know. I can't do everything, and honestly, it's a little bit terrifying."

"Nobody expects you to do everything. You're too hard on yourself. You're a better best friend than I am," I admit.

"That's because you're a guy, Mitchell. Nobody expects you to take care of someone else's dying wishes."

"What's that supposed to mean?" I pretend as if she's hurt my feelings when we both know that she hasn't.

"There's something I've been thinking about. On Paisley's list, that is. Number four is to go on a vacation with my best friends. Do you think that's something she's still capable of doing given her sickness?"

"If she's put on there get drunk at a beach bonfire, we can take her on a friend vacation."

"Where do you see that?"

"Number five." I point at the sheet of paper in front of me as if Georgia can see it through the phone, and she laughs.

"Can cancer patients drink?"

"What's the worst thing that will happen if she does? Is she going to die? Oh, no." I put on my best sarcastic voice with the last two words. I suspect Georgia is thinking about slapping me, and I silently thank God for her not being able to reach through the receiver.

"You're too morbid, Mitchell."

"No, really. Think about it. We could mix those two things into one trip. Paisley doesn't say that we have to take her across the ocean or even across the country. I mean, when's the last time you've been to Partridge Island? It's what, a couple of hours from here? Red beaches, lots of places for bonfires. Good old country living."

I roll my computer chair over to the bed and lean over to rummage for the pack of smokes Dean left down there the last time he was over. The phone gets squished between my ear and my shoulder, the device being held awkwardly so I can hear.

"You might be on to something," Georgia replies, in agreement. "Kind of a little last hurrah before we're all split up until Thanksgiving?"

"Something like that."

She's thinking much too far into the future. I don't think Paisley's going to make it all the way until Thanksgiving, but I don't bother to press the issue or bring up the likelihood of the scenario. I don't want to think about it or admit it.

"Yes, something like that."

"I'm going to call Dean," she asserts, her natural in-charge voice back on the line. "Then, Taryn. Don't tell Paisley anything yet until we have confirmation this is going to go down. I'll talk to you later, all right?"

"All right," I reply, locating the crumpled cardboard package from behind a discarded shoebox. "Later, G."

Georgia hangs up without saying goodbye, while I pop out a cigarette from the leftover collection of Dean's smokes. I rise from the chair and plunk myself down by the open window, staring at Paisley's empty bedroom. With a flick of my finger on the lighter, I light the stick, dragging on the smoke in a soulful silence, watching the streetlamps all flicker on with the lack of solar power. A collection of constellations starts to prick through the inky fabric of the night, and even though I can't name a single one, someday Paisley's going to be up there, twinkling down on us and laughing her ass off.

FOUR

~ MITCHELL ~

Three days comes and goes, and everyone is still alive.

That's not saying much in general terms, but for the status of our group of friends, that's very much a positive note. The worst part about the end of the week has been that the prep girls have somehow used their skills in deduction to figure out that I'm going to prom. They seem to have decided that dividing up each of the predicted eight slow dances is the way to go, crooning next to my locker about the way men look in suits, kind of like a younger version of James Bond, which is a blasphemous statement to the work of Ian Fleming, if you ask me. Of course, nobody did ask me, so I guess it seems kind of like a compliment.

To my own demise, I presumed telling them that I was taking Paisley as a date would be a deterrent, but instead, it seems to have attracted them more. I guess now I'm 'honestly a really nice guy,' as opposed to whatever I was earlier. I liked it better when people assumed I was a quiet asshole.

Needless to say, I'm ready to take off on vacation with the only four people who don't want to crawl all over me. I've practically already packed my bag with all my summer essentials for a perfect Canada Day weekend: shorts, sandals, and a graduation bottle of

Jack Daniel's Nolan slipped me on his visit home a few weekends past. And when I say that I've packed my things, I mean that I've done it in my head; my gym bag remains balled up in the bottom of my closet back behind where I found my shoes for prom and the matching red tie.

An hour before I'm supposed to pick up Paisley, I'm sitting in my bedroom in my boxers, hemming my dress pants, because it turns out Nolan is about five inches longer in the leg than I am. I've scrounged up Mom's sewing kit from the basement, in secret, of course, putting my home economics skills to moderate use with floppy lines and poor stitching. At least I remembered to make sure the thread matches the pants, which is probably an indicator of success if there happened to be one for a matter of this magnitude.

I'm just about to tie off the thread on my left pant leg when my phone buzzes from the desk and I stab myself in the finger.

Goddamnit.

Georgia: *I just had a brilliant idea.*

Georgia. Always coming up with the best plans and spurting them out at the most inconvenient times.

Mitchell: *What now?*

Georgia: *Did you know there's a ferry that takes you from Partridge Island to Hemlock Cove?*

Mitchell: *What the hell's Hemlock Cove?*

Georgia: *Google it, Mitchell. Jesus. I'm not an encyclopedia. Don't worry; I'll wait.*

I sigh even though Georgia can't hear me, squashing the fabric of the pants on my lap as I flip open the lid to my laptop. The computer whirs as I tuck my final stitch into place, knotting the thread with my bumpy fingers and biting off the end of the string with my teeth. There's a little, wet spot on the hem from my mouth, but if someone's that close to my feet, it better be because they've better have fallen over drunk or I'm kicking them for staring at Paisley in that gorgeous red dress.

As the starting screen loads up, I slip the grey material over my legs and stare at myself in the full-length mirror mounted on my closet door.

Good enough.

I sit back at the desk and look at my phone, but Georgia hasn't followed up. She's waiting for me to search the damn place and let her know my opinion.

A quick search gives me more information than I could ever possibly want to know. The only factoids that I need are that the Cove is a part of the Gulf of Saint Lawrence, the primary language is French, one of the most popular pastimes is windsurfing, and it takes five hours to get there by boat.

Georgia's light bulb moment comes over to greet me, and I dig that crumpled piece of paper from my desk, unraveling the folded sections. Number seven on Paisley's list is to travel by boat, and number nine is to try an extreme sport. Combined with the list item about speaking French, maybe Georgia is on to something here.

Mitchell: *You might be a genius—but how long do you figure we're going to be able to take off for? Half the summer?*

Georgia: *Thank you for finally admitting that fact. And I figured it was open-ended. We'll come back when Paisley gets too sick to function. What do you say? The others are already on board.*

Mitchell: *I say we do it. I've got extra money saved for school that I'd much rather use for something like this.*

Georgia: *That's my boy. See you soon. We'll talk details.*

As I place my phone back down on the desk to pop on a set of dress socks, there's a knock on my door.

"Yeah?" I close the lid of my computer and stuff the paper with Paisley's list back into my desk, just as Mom pokes her head through. She beams as she gets a good look at me—or maybe she has on just a touch too much highlighting makeup.

"You decent?"

"I have pants on if that's what you mean. Plus you're already in here so asking the question kind of defeats the purpose."

She ignores my sassy mouth.

"Look at you, Mitchell. You look just like your father did on the day I married him. So handsome," she croons, her tone of voice reminds me a little too much of the popular girls. "Is Paisley going to come over so we can get some photos? Poor dove. She can't be much longer for this world."

Mom wiggles my tie back and forth, tightening it on my neck to the point where I consider if she's actually trying to strangle me.

"I told her I'd go pick her up. I'm sure her mother will take some." I immediately loosen the tie, oxygen hitting my lungs as if I had previously been drowning. Mom looks less than impressed with that idea, but she doesn't protest. She learned long ago that we Anders men are tough to crack and a little bit stubborn. After all, she is entirely outnumbered. Instead, she takes a seat on the edge of my bed, smoothing out the creases and eyeing the sewing kit.

"Paisley's lucky she has such wonderful friends. Especially a boy who actually hemmed his own pants for her."

I smile, staring down at the floor.

"Mom, speaking of Paisley. Georgia's kind of come up with this plan." I hesitate in saying the words because if there's a way to poke holes in Georgia's plan, my mother will find a way to do so.

"Oh? What kind of plan?"

I toy with the closure clasp of the sewing kit.

"Well, Paisley's got this list. Georgia helped her make it. It's kind of like all the last things she wants to do."

"A bucket list?"

"Yeah, you know what I mean," I say with a nod. Everyone knows what a bucket list is. I don't know why I didn't just say that in the first place. "Anyway, Georgia's figured out a way we can make most of the list happen. We were thinking about taking Paisley to Partridge Island for a little while. Then Georgia mentioned the Hemlock Cove—"

Mom holds up one hand. "Mitchell, you do remember the girl is sick, right?"

"I just—" I try to speak, but she interrupts me again.

"It's a really sweet thing you all are thinking about doing, but you might want to talk to Paisley's mother first. What if Paisley gets worse while she's away? What if she passes on? Do you guys know what to do if something like that were to happen?"

No. I don't. I have no idea.

"Mom, we're not kids anymore..."

"Mitchell, honey. It's not about being kids. And if you think that's all this is about then you might want to re-evaluate. If Paisley's mother sees no problem with it, then go ahead. But don't make plans without including her family. They're the ones with the most to lose here."

"Don't you think Paisley has the most to lose? Think about everything she's going to miss out on." A little bit of teenage angst rises in my throat as if I'm being told I'm not allowed to do something.

"I am thinking about it," Mom begins. "But please don't argue. As you said, you're not kids anymore, and you're dealing with some very adult issues. You need to manage them respectfully."

Mom rises from the bed, looking me over with a careful gaze that makes me uncomfortable. There's a little sparkle in her eye, a thought maybe, something she's got in her mind but she isn't saying aloud because she's only just realized it.

"What?" I hand her back the sewing kit and pick up my suit jacket.

"Do you love her, Mitchell?"

I'm so shocked by the question I have no words, my mouth opening and closing like a goldfish. The reaction seems to please her.

"There's no right answer here. If you do, you're running out of time. If you don't, you're still running out of time. It's lovely you want to make the most of this. If you love the girl, please don't be modest about it. You've known each other since you were small children. Now isn't the time for games or silly romance. If you love her—I mean, really love her, Mitchell—you give that girl everything for as long as she's still here on God's green earth."

Mom cradles the little box in her arms as if it's the most precious thing she's ever held.

My heart is screaming, looking down at the desk, piles of colored photos of wildflowers scattered over the surface as I push them around with my fingers to find the one with the red roses.

Shit. I'm in love with a girl who is going to die.

"Your silence just answered your own question," Mom replies quietly, snapping the lid of the sewing kit open and shut over and over. "You know what you have to do now. Just don't be too scared to do it because you'll always regret it. And it's not like you can go back and fix what you didn't do or say what you forgot."

"I know," I state, flicking her edge of the photo. The red reminds me of Paisley's dress, the color of her lips, and the redness of my face as I've been thinking about her in a more-than-friends way for quite some time.

Mom stands, making her way back to the door.

"Don't underestimate what you have to give her, honey. But also don't overestimate how long you have to provide it. You're walking a very thin line."

"That's not helping me feel any better. It's just stressing me out."

She places her hand on the doorknob, her carefully manicured fingernails tapping on the metal.

"Love is stressful, Mitchell. But I promise you it's worth it. Your father and I ended up with you and Nolan, and we couldn't be more proud of the men you're growing up into. It takes a strong person to admit that someone means something to them. It takes an even stronger one to do so when they have an expiry date."

My mother offers me a little smile, and I lean back in my desk chair with nothing else to say. She's right—of course, Mom's always right in these situations—but I don't know if I'm the kind of person she sees me as. My heart and my head are panicky; frozen at the thought of giving my heart to Paisley only to have it eventually be buried with her.

For a few minutes, I am lost, staring at the picture of the rose when my phone buzzes next to me and vibrates all the way over to hit a stack of papers.

Nolan: *Have fun at prom, dork.*

Mitchell: *Thanks, Nolan. Have fun getting blackout drunk with your frat buddies.*

Nolan: *I'll be home in a few weeks once my job placement is over. I'll teach you how to shotgun a beer like a good brother should.*

I don't bother telling Nolan that I already know how to do that, because as I go to reply to his message, it hits me that I'm late to pick up Paisley.

FIVE

~ PAISLEY ~

Overnight and deep into the pits of the early morning is the time when the cancer is the worst.

I'm more than aware that's not possible, that it's the same and yet progressively worse as the seconds tick past in my life, turning minutes to smoke and hours to ashes. However, it feels like those wee hours of the evening are the ones that last the longest, keeping me awake with migraines and shortness of breath and the stars in my eyes like I have when I stand up too fast. I often find myself crushed up against the surface of my memory foam mattress, begging for either air or death, whichever one is willing to come first.

Air, always air. But someday, death. I just don't know which day, and that's the real killer.

But not today. That death won't be today, and that crushed up feeling won't be tonight because I'm going to prom, an event I wasn't even sure I was going to live long enough to be a part of.

I spend longer getting ready than I ever have for anything else in my whole life, trying to take away from my pallid and sickly appearance. Hours and layers of makeup later, I find myself standing awkwardly in my living room, feeling the fabric of the red dress brush against my bare legs while I watch for the headlights of Mitchell's Ford Escape. Mom's in the kitchen cooking up something with bacon, at least a pound of it in and on the oven, in anticipation for my father's return home from a rig somewhere down past Texas. Although he hadn't quite made the vacation request in time to see me head off to prom, he had always promised he would make it home for graduation. I'm an only child, and apparently, something about graduating from high school makes for a big deal in the world of parents.

I don't get it, but then again I'm not a parent.

My stomach does a flip as the daytime running lights of the SUV break over the glass of the bay living room window, fracturing my fragmented thoughts.

"Is that Mitchell?" Mom calls, coming out of the kitchen, wiping her hands on a dish towel at the same time as the oven timer beeps.

"Yeah," I mumble, my voice breaking in the middle as I watch a nearly unidentifiable, well-groomed man step out of the vehicle, a crimson tie fluttering across his broad chest inside an open grey suit jacket. It takes me a second to realize the figure is Mitchell, even though it appears out of his own car, a slim and trim two-piece attire hugging his newly acquired physique. Mom looks over my shoulder, pushing the curtains away, oblivious to my panicked drooling.

"Wow, that boy really knows how to wear a suit, doesn't he?"

"Mom!" The word crackles from my throat, the skin inside parched in my forgetfulness of swallowing. I quickly shove the strange feelings down into my toes, trying to keep the bubbles of intensity from boiling over. "It's just Mitchell. You know, that guy I've known since I was five. He used to throw me off the deck into the snow. Don't make a big deal out of this."

Mom drops the curtain and stares at me as I watch him stride over the cobblestone driveway.

"Oh, Paisley. If only you could see your face right now." She grins from ear to ear.

"What? What's wrong with my face?"

Grabbing my shoulders, she shuffles me away from the window in haste, the twinging of an idea trickling over her expression.

"I need to know something, Paisley. Is there something going on with Mitchell and you?"

The question floors me, and for a second I can't speak. A million little thoughts run through my head in an anxious rush. Okay, so maybe I've had a dream a time or two where things between Mitchell and me got a little bit heated, but that was in my head while I was sleeping and there was nothing I could do about it.

"Of course not." I can't even tell if I'm lying.

She drops her hands to her sides.

"I guess then I don't need to remind you of the kinds of complications that could cause. But I don't want you to miss out on life just because of your diagnosis, Paisley. You should still try your hardest to be as you are right now. Mitchell understands that."

"Are you trying to tell me that there should be something going on between us?"

There's a knock at the door, reminding us that company's waiting on the other side. Ivy starts to bark as soon as she sees Mitchell through the door-side window.

"I'm trying to tell you that I see what's going on in your head even though you're not using your words to express it. And Mitchell's going to see it too, so you'd better sort out what you want with him going forward because your relationship is going to get a lot more complicated after tonight."

Seamlessly, she pulls open the front door as if we weren't just having a conversation.

"Mitchell! You look fantastic. Is that one of Nolan's suits? I remember when the two of you used only to be so high."

"Hi, Mrs. Watts." There's a gravelly undertone to Mitchell's voice that I swear wasn't there earlier in the day, and he leans down to pet Ivy. "Hemmed it myself, he's still the tall one in the family. Kind of a last minute thing as I'm sure you're aware."

"I'm just pleased that Paisley's able to go. I'll never forget going to my prom with Roger all those years ago." Mom gets a daydreamy look on her face, and I take the cue as my moment to walk into the entryway.

Mitchell looks even better up close.

"Anyway," she continues, half of her previous sentence not having to even registered with me. "I need to get a couple of pictures of the two of you before I let you leave this house. I'll let you two say hello and—for God's sake, Paisley, put on some shoes and meet me out in the front garden. We can get some nice photos next to the latticework." She grabs her camera, already prepped on the entryway table, and flings the storm door open in all her glory, letting in the warm June air and a rush of sunshine.

I don't say anything until she's off the front porch.

"Nice suit."

I'm an idiot, but Mitchell doesn't seem to care.

"Dress looks better in person."

Casting my eyes downward, hips to toes, my cerise toenails poke out from beneath the hem. Unsure of what to do with the compliment, instead I just start talking. I'm nervous. I'm never nervous around Mitchell.

"I didn't have time to get shoes. I figure the dress is long enough nobody will know what's on my feet anyway. I'm a little too unsteady to be walking around in heels."

"Well." Mitchell takes a seat on the hallway bench. "What are our options?"

I hike up my dress and dump a wicker basket of footwear on the welcome mat.

"Black flats, nude flats, denim flats," I begin, tossing the pairs back into the basket. "Polka dot flats, one brown flat, a pair of beach flip flops from The Boat Shop and my old pink high tops from junior high. The latter still have our signatures all over them."

"My vote's on the high tops. Good memories in those shoes. We need to make some good memories right about now."

"Oh God, Mitchell. Don't you be the one to start getting soft on me tonight. Can we please just forget that I'm going to die here any day and have a normal evening like regular high school kids do?" I ask the question even though removing the reality behind it is next to impossible.

"Are we, though?" He stares dead at me.

"Are we what?"

"Regular high school kids?"

I think it over, plopping down on the step and likely wrinkling my dress.

"I guess not."

There's a moment of sustained silence, then casual laughter between us breaks the tension.

"You look fantastic, really." Mitchell smiles as I lace up my shoes. "Kind of a sultry edge about you. I'm not used to you presenting yourself that way. It's kind of—I don't know the right word. Alarming is the only one that comes to mind. Guess we're not little kids anymore. It's honestly a little bit scary."

I clomp my foot down on the tile, wiggling my toes behind the pink canvas.

"Mom thinks you look good in a suit."

Mitchell's face turns a burning shade of red as he puts out his hand to help me off the step.

"What do you think?"

We stare at each other in an infinite moment of frozen feelings and immortality. It's a loaded question with so many possible repercussions. What is it that I think? He looks fantastic; we have history, I'm dying, I hate that I can't stop thinking about him. On top of that, we're running short on time; fate and time and life and existence are working against us.

But I don't say any of that.

Oh, no. That would be too easy. That would give him permission to break my heart when my other organs are already failing.

"We'd better get going, or we're going to be late."

Mitchell's shoulders almost imperceptibly slump.

The answer in my head is the answer he wanted, which tells me something else entirely.

He isn't going to let me get away with avoiding the question, because we're deep in a cat-and-mouse game now and apparently we're both more than aware of it. The way he looks at me, raising his eyebrow with a half-smile creates a warbling feeling in the pit of my stomach, forcing a heat wave to rush up my body and into my cheeks. I've never noticed that dimple on his right cheek before, but I'm sure seeing it now, and maybe that tiny mole next to his nose was always there, or it's just decided to make an appearance at this moment.

"Come on, you two!" My mother calls from out in the garden, breaking the glance that Mitchell and I have been holding. "I at least want to get one nice picture to show your father since he can't be here."

Mitchell's face flushes gently, something I wouldn't have noticed if I wasn't looking for it, and he averts his eyes.

"Guess we'd better go do this then, Songbird."

"Yeah," I reply, my voice quiet but my mind racing. "I just can't believe it's happening."

And I can't believe that Mitchell and I are in the throes of something that should probably and logically be nothing at all.

After seventeen minutes, we finally convince my mother that she has enough photographs to last several lifetimes, and we are dismissed to hop into Mitchell's Ford Escape and make a getaway for the school. The windows are down and blowing the June air through the vehicle, tossing the strands of my wig every which way and making me feel alive. A bumblebee floats through the car window slow motion, humming a tune I can't understand in a language I never bothered to learn. It twirls about inside for a few seconds before realizing the directional mistake and going back the way it came from. Mitchell and I are doing the same thing; buzzing around each other with hints. The dying part of my life is taking a toll on the benefits of living.

We drive to the school without feeling the need for conversation, the radio playing something from the early 1990's that I can't remember the name of. Mitchell must smoke fifty cigarettes if he smokes a single one, lighting the sticks up in sequence as we head through the main road, sucking them down as if he requires them to breathe. There's a lot of nerves and anxiety coursing through him, and I work through various attempts to rationalize his feelings while I'm sure he sits over on the other side of the car and thinks about nothing at all. I've always had a tendency to over-analyze, while Mitchell's been the one throughout my life who takes the time to show me that not everything has to have a reason. Sometimes things just are.

He parks the Escape at the back of the lot, the only space left in front of the building since we're already at least fifteen minutes late arriving. If anyone asked, I'm sure he would try to explain that the set starting hour of prom has always been more of a suggestion than a necessity.

"What are you thinking?" Mitchell finally asks as he turns off the ignition and the rumbling of the SUV quiets.

"Honestly?" I brush a piece of wig hair from my face and run my fingers through the ends to tidy them, using the movement as a distraction from my anxiety at the question. "I think you— I don't know. I think maybe tonight is the first night it's come to me that this list thing is real. Like, it's all I have left. It's really just a long farewell list of ideas."

There's a window of silence as Mitchell takes a deep breath with a muted grin.

"Here I thought that you couldn't get over how attractive I am in Nolan's old suit."

A tiny snort escapes my throat as I burst into laughter.

"Well, there's always that. That's less morbid to think about."

"Just think of it this way," Mitchell pronounces. "At least you know what you want to do with the rest of your life. I still have no idea. That's scary in its own way and growing up with no direction whatsoever. It's nothing in comparison, but what I'm trying to say is that you're not the only one who is walking around terrified. We're all terrified of something. Your something is just bigger than ours."

He places his hand on mine, the warmth of his palm spreading across my fingers and up my arm, just as Taryn slams her hand on the hood of the Escape. The sound makes me jump, and she laughs, her long hair tied up in a mass of waves. Looking up, Georgia is waving from across the campus, running toward us in a bright gold dress while Dean trails along, contemplative, looking dashing in his black tuxedo.

"Hey!" G's voice travels across the murmur of the school, bright sun shining hot on her dark brown hair. "You guys ready to go in? I'm so excited to see how the decorations look all lit up. Plus we have to get a photo together at the booth!" There's a pretty sparkle to her face, maybe from the sun and perhaps from the make-up, but whatever it is, gives her the gentle glow of an excited teenager.

"You girls go in," Dean starts, letting Georgia loose. "I forgot my smokes in the car. Mitchell, leave the ladies alone for a minute and walk with me."

"We'll meet you inside!" She tosses the words over her shoulder as we stride through the collection of classmates and their families, the crowds dwindling slowly.

Music pulses through my core, and I feel a bit like dancing, the music and pulsating darkness swallowing me whole, as if I'm a pill in a series of medications that need to be consumed in a hurry before it dissolves. Taryn's decorations are magical; the inspiration she went with was Van Gogh's Starry Night, and so the Prom Committee decked out the gymnasium and adjacent hallways in indigo and silver fabrics, battery-powered fairy lights are strewn across the ceiling and down the corridors. Mason jars with fake candles flicker in the dim atmosphere, one per table in the atrium, with a punch bowl in the center, plastic cups, and buckets of ice with bottled water free for the taking. The shop class made a trellis for the doorway between the rooms, fake ivy leaves and ivory fabric draped just so.

"Wow, Taryn. You really went all out."

I snort at Georgia's outdated expression while a gaggle of students I'll likely never see again croon over the array and snap selfies in front of the fabric drops. A heavy bass line crashes through the doorway straight ahead, white lights spiraling along the walls and mesmerizing me until Mitchell and Dean appear at my side.

"So listen, Paisley. We've got something we want to tell you." Georgia looks for confirmation from Mitchell who wordlessly gives her the go ahead. "We kind of tried to plan this post-prom, post-graduation trip for you to do all the things left on your list."

My face is going to crack open since I'm smiling so wide.

"Oh my God, are you guys serious? That's amazing! Even the party on the beach? And the boat? Where are we going?" The words come out of my mouth faster and louder, rivaling the beat of the background music. Mitchell looks like he wants to sink into the rhythm and never be let out again while Dean looks like he could use one of those cigarettes in his pocket right about now.

"Well, that's the downside, Ley. We aren't going anywhere. Your mom said that it was too reckless since you're so sick." Georgia chooses her words carefully, but there's a broken undertone in there. That's the way they all feel; the subculture of their existence in the time leading up to the world after me.

"Oh," I reply, in a voice so small I suspect my friends can hardly hear it. "I just thought that maybe I'd actually get to finish my list. Mark off some of those things I'm bound to miss with you guys, you know. Hell, I just wanted to forget that I'm sick for a while and do all that ridiculous bullshit you can only get away with when you're eighteen."

I choke, a clump of letters stuck in my throat, and tears start to well up in my eyes for just a second until Georgia pulls me close.

"This must be so hard for you." Georgia's words muffle against my wig. "We really tried. It wasn't anything crazy, but it was something."

I push away, rubbing the wet lines off my face with one hand.

"No, nobody knows what this must be like for me," I start, the hue of the red dress likely matching my frustrated complexion. "I walk around, and everyone looks at me as if I'm a dog on death row, some discarded poor thing nobody knows how to fix, but they don't want to break. Maybe I want to be broken. Maybe I'm not scared to death to die. Maybe the only thing I'm worried about is that I'm not going to get to live anymore because I'm practically already dead."

"That's so not true, Paisley. We can do so many things even if we just stay here." Taryn offers the best compromise she can, a chatty group of preppy seniors walking past us heading inside to dance. They check Mitchell out for so long I swear they're devouring him with their eyes and it makes me want to punch each one of them in their perfectly made-up faces.

"That's the thing, Taryn. I'm always here. I've always been here. I want to see something other than one town. I want someone to remember me for doing something great. I don't want to be that girl who had cancer. I want to be the girl who took a road trip a month—a week—a *day* before she died and stood on top of the world and screamed at God to take her because she's finally ready to go back home. I want to see the stars from somewhere with red sand and cliffs and the rush of the waves. I want to stand on the ocean. I want to tell cancer to go screw itself because even though it can take my life, it can't stop me from living."

With those words, I stomp under the archway and disappear into the blackness of the indoor starry night.

SIX

~ PAISLEY ~

Bodies crash around me to the tune of a newish dance hit, silhouettes waving and swerving along with the timed rhythm.

I stand outside of it all, absorbing the magnitude of my own mother's denial as hot tears welling up in the corner of my eyes and bracing to smudge my eye makeup. I could scream at the top of my lungs, and I don't think anyone would hear over the electronic melody. The thought crosses my mind, but instead, it wells up like a knot in my chest, trying to suffocate me.

My whole list is out there waiting for me.

I deserve to have these experiences, I tell myself. What I don't deserve is someone telling me how I should spend the final days of my life. I'm the one dying; everyone else gets to go on without me, and it's terrible, and I hate it, and it makes me want to throw myself out a fifteenth story window just to get it over with.

The pounding fades, the upbeat song switching to something slower, and I watch from the sidelines as groups of students couple off with their dates. Hands carefully wrap around waists and necks, quiet words whispered loudly in each other's ears like desperate little promise rings that only last until something better comes along. I swear I almost hear the plans for the future being made and

I can't help but consider if any one of them will be like me, and not be permitted to have a future at all.

I sense Mitchell behind me before processing he's there, knowing his presence just by the way the feel of the room changes around him. There's something in my body that knows when he's nearby, a prickling on the back of my neck that seeps into the part of my brain that isn't covered in cancer. My theory is confirmed by a touch on my arm, fingers curving around my elbow to hand me a small piece of paper.

"I didn't get to give you your flower. I almost forgot."

Sucking down impending tears, I turn to face the boy behind me, putting on the bravest face I can muster despite my breakdown.

"It reminded me of your dress." His voice is low in my ear and makes the tips of my fingers tingle. "And of the way it makes you look. Beautiful, but a little bit dangerous."

He's trying to make me feel better with pretty words and delicate lies, and it's working.

I slip the paper out from Mitchell's fingers, the page small and carefully cut down from a larger piece of photo stock. On it, he's placed a close-up shot of a startlingly red rose, minuscule water droplets lining the surface of the flower. It appears to be a spring morning, a new bloom, with a dark background and an impending storm. The dichotomy in the shot is spectacular.

"You're ridiculous." I sniffle, incredulous that he printed me out a photo of a flower just as I asked. "Thank you. I didn't think you'd actually take the time to do this. I honestly didn't expect anything. This is sweet of you."

"It's just a stock photo, Paisley. It's not a big deal."

It's a big deal to me. When your days are numbered, everything becomes a big deal. But I don't get to say that because Mitchell keeps talking.

"Listen," Mitchell starts, trying to rationalize with me over the acoustic version of a song I almost recognize. "We can't give you exactly what you wanted, but Georgia tried really hard to put something together. Trust me; she's disappointed too. If there was anything else we could do, you know we would do it. But instead of dwelling on those thoughts and trying to come up with a game plan right now, we need to just make the most of this night while we still all have each other."

The electric laser lights make designs on Mitchell's shirt, waving slow strips of ivory back and forth in no particular pattern. The suggestion is morbid, a reminder of the nearing of my end of days. I appreciate the honesty, and he definitely has a point. Thinking, I run my eyes over at the little picture of the rose again, brushing the edges with my fingertips and smiling at the sensitive nature of the boy in front of me.

We stand amidst the slow music, staring through and into each other, and all at once the understanding hits me as to what those other girls have been going on about. It comes to me in slow motion, a gentle cognizance of my own emotions, and I am pricked with curiosity over what kissing Mitchell might be like. I picture something soft and perfect, outside of this room in a quiet moment by ourselves, where we have time to enjoy the magnitude of the action.

"Paisley?"

We've been staring at each other for a long time, much too long for friends.

"I don't have anywhere to put my flower."

The statement feels stupid, but the only other thing I think of doing right now is kissing Mitchell and telling him I can't believe I didn't realize sooner that I'm woefully attracted to him.

He laughs.

"Here, I'll keep it in my pocket. You can pin it on your mood board when you get home. A little souvenir of the night someone finally dragged me out of my house." Mitchell slips the small photo into his jacket liner. "Now come dance with me before this song is over, and we have to flail around awkwardly to a ridiculous beat."

"You're so romantic, Mitchell." There's a sarcastic lilt to my voice as I sniff again, delicately rubbing itchy leftover tears from my face. "No wonder all these girls want you."

Mitchell snorts and chuckles at the same time, making the same noise as my dog does when her nose is stuffed up.

"Isn't it unfortunate I don't want them? Life's just not fair."

He's right. Life's a bitch.

Taking me by the hand, Mitchell twirls me out into an empty spot on the dance floor. The clumps of students collected somewhere to the center of the gymnasium barely make a dent in the number of people permitted in the space as per fire regulations, music washing over top of the swirling figurines. I breathe in the smell of Mitchell's soap and clean cologne, trying to immerse my lungs in his essence without making it visible I'm falling fast and hard.

There's no awkwardness as he pulls me close to him—we've danced at school events from junior high up until now—but there's a purposeful sigh that presses his chest against mine just for a second. That's long enough for me to know that he's finally unclenched his jaw, feeling safe enough to relax.

Mitchell would never admit it to anyone, but I suspect he doesn't go to things like this very often because the gatherings make him anxious. The crowds, the new attention from the other girls, the loud sounds and dark spaces. Ever since we were young I've had the feeling he harbors emotions deeper than the four of us can understand, and as we turn in a slow and steady circle, I toss the idea around in my head if sometime after I'm gone he will finally grow into himself and come to terms with it all.

I hope he does. He deserves to be happy.

The last notes of the song play and I still can't place the title, acoustics fading into a rocking bass replacement that should jolt us from our moment. Instead, a feeling starts in the corner of my eyes, an aura of fuzzy stars and bursts of non-existent sunbeams. It feels like someone's stuck the back end of a hammer into the base of my skull and is pulling out my brain as if it were a nail in a gyprock wall. I barely have any warning before my knees get weak, and I collapse all my weight into Mitchell's arms.

"Paisley?"

He says my name, but his voice sounds very far away and underwater, all gurgling and sloshing as if I were being towed away underneath it. I try to respond, but I'm in a haze, blinking rapidly to try and get the sparks out of my field of vision. Mitchell must be able to tell I'm still coherent because he keeps talking, muffled words in a language I can't comprehend, little shadows of his syllables snaking around the gymnasium. Then I'm being carried, probably not very elegantly, back into the candlelit atrium. The blobs in my vision start to fade, as fast as they appeared.

"Jesus, what happened?" Taryn's voice comes through as plain as day, and her footsteps echo in my head as she prances across the industrial tile. "Paisley? Can you hear me?"

"She's having an episode. I need to set her down somewhere."

There's scraping and then a minute later my touch on Mitchell turns into dead air and a cold arm.

"Do we call her mom? Is this serious? I'll find Georgia, she knows about this kind of thing. I mean, she has to. Her dad's a doctor." Taryn spits out words frantically, her little yellow dress blasting holes in my eye sockets as I am slammed with thirty seconds of the worst migraine I've ever experienced.

"Find a teacher first, then Georgia. Someone with actual life experience might know what to do." Mitchell's voice is firm, but the corners of it are worried and tattered.

"Wait..." I drop the word, and it tumbles from my lips to an empty tile beneath one of Taryn's fake ivy plants. I spit it out as I hold in my nausea. "It's okay. This happens sometimes. If I sit, it goes away."

I swear every letter of every word I speak balances in the air in front of me before they pop like alphabet balloons. Within seconds, everything goes back to normal.

"I'm okay." I take a deep breath. I'm not okay, I'm an idiot, but

I don't want anyone to know that. I want to go back into that dark room and pretend like someday one of these episodes isn't going to be the end.

Mitchell looks less than convinced, but he extends his hand, and shakily I place my fingers into his grasp.

"Let's go find Georgia and Dean and get this party started."

I nod, using Mitchell's strength to hold me up as I make a valiant attempt at standing.

"Careful, please God, don't hurt yourself," Taryn states, holding me by the other arm. "Are you sure you're okay to go back in there?"

My eyes are a little bit fuzzy as I stand, a touch of vertigo hitting me, but I don't want to let either of them know that something still isn't quite right. This is prom for Christ's sake; we're supposed to be having fun and dancing and remembering all the stupid things we did in high school, not worrying about whether or not my brain is going to attack me.

"I'm fine," I promise. The look on Mitchell's blurry face says that he doesn't believe me, but all he does is tighten his grip on my body and lean his side into my shoulder for support. I am thankful for his careful understanding, and I press into the fabric of Nolan's suit and try to melt through to feel Mitchell's skin underneath the cloth.

I want this boy. I want all of him, and I never want to let him go.

SEVEN

~ MITCHELL ~

Prom night fades into a blanket of milky stars, the inside of the school weaving and melting into a replica of the atmosphere outdoors.

Gradually, the energy of the night diminishes, the water bottles in the ice buckets are all consumed, and the all-night dance turns into a sleepless night of quiet tunes and cornered conversations. Yawning students disperse in tiny droves, some to after-parties and others home to their beds where they will fall asleep in full faces of makeup and hair full of product. The morning will be an awakening of a different kind, a day of rest before graduation is upon us and we head into the last carefree summer of our entire lives.

We can't forget about the fact that Paisley's going to die without ever having the opportunity to finish the things on her list. We don't talk about it when she's around—that only seems like cruel torture —but the scheming comes out in rushed intervals and hands-to-ears. Just as we're about to call it a night, Dean ready to take Taryn and Georgia back home, Georgia gets a text from her father that could potentially solve all of our problems. That is if Paisley's mother agrees to it.

Taryn and Dean are carrying on with some conversation about

a video game release and Paisley's in the washroom when Georgia's phone beeps. She wrangles it from the pocket of her clutch, the contents stuffed with mints and perfume to cover the smell of Dean's cigarettes, and reads it silently before showing the screen to me.

Doctor Hart: *Hey Georgia Peach—I booked into a medical conference on Partridge Island for next week. Any interest in coming to hang out on the Island? Not much to do but lots of beaches. Maybe one of your friends would want to tag along.*

"Are you thinking what I'm thinking?" she asks with a tired smile.

"Do you think Mrs. Watts would go for it? I mean, your dad's a doctor after all, what better way to mitigate the whole medical emergency scenario than by having your own personal attendant?"

"What's going on?" Taryn asks, pulling an errant bobby pin out from her hair and flipping off her shoes again to press the soles of her feet against the cold tile.

"Georgia's dad is going to the Island. Maybe we could try Paisley's mom again?"

"It's worth a shot," Dean shrugs with a stifled yawn. "Worst option is that she'll just say no."

"Maybe throw the plan out at your dad first, G. See what he has to say about it." Taryn interrupts my musing. "If he answers fast enough, we can text Mitchell, and maybe he can drop a hint when he brings Paisley home."

A valid point, and an easy way to keep me from having to badger the same idea into Mrs. Watts' head. She's always had a liking for me in particular, and maybe the kindness of taking her dying daughter to prom will offer some leniency in the circumstances. It's crude and selfish but it's also the best we can hope for.

Paisley emerges from the washroom with a pale face and tired candor. Her black bob doesn't seem as smooth as it did previously, a little tousled on the ends from all the dancing she's been doing.

"Ready to go then?" She offers me a weak little smile. "Sorry for taking off so early, you guys. I hope you have fun at Melanie M's lake party. I just think I've had enough excitement and disappointment for one night."

Sometimes you can tell more about a person by the reactions they get from others than the way they react to situations on their own. In our case, Dean has a quirky grin on his face and Taryn's very obviously trying to stifle her desire to say something about Georgia's father and the conference on Partridge Island. Georgia herself is the only one who is managing to hold it all together, aside from myself of course. And even then, I probably have a terrible poker face. Nolan used to be able to tell when I was lying all the time.

"All right then. I'll talk to you guys later?" I put a little emphasis on the word later, as if they might not understand what I'm hinting at. Taryn winks at me as she and Georgia hug Paisley goodbye, all mushed together in a puddle of girls.

"Thanks for helping me with the decorations, Ley. You look beautiful. Have a good night."

"Thanks, Tee." Paisley leans on my shoulder and I lean back, half to support her tired body and the other half because I just want to touch her. "I'll talk to you in the morning."

We amble down the hallway with our arms entwined, passing the leftover decorations that haven't been destroyed from the wandering fingers of students and the haphazard leaning of bodies against the rows of lockers. I pull the car keys from my pocket, the jingling sound barely perceptible between the sound of music and the laughter of sleepy students, and Paisley stifles a yawn with her opposite hand.

"Did you have fun, at least?" I hold open the front door of the school, letting in the dark, warm air of the night. "Other than the disappointment of finding out there's no trip and the part where you almost passed out on me."

Paisley has this delicate laugh that melts directly into the lining of my stomach.

"Of course. Thank you for agreeing to come with me."

"You say that like it was something horrible. I wanted to come with you."

My confession is punctuated by the sound of our feet swishing across the grass field of the front lawn, little dewdrops covering our shoes and the hems of our clothes. Paisley wraps her fingers in the material of her dress so she doesn't trip over it, her bare legs pale in the moonlight, and she doesn't say anything as we approach the car. The rear lights blink on and off with the automatic key fob as I press the button to unlock the vehicle, making bright little spots in my line of vision. We take our seats, me as driver and Paisley as a passenger, and the slam of the doors explode out into the silent night. I can't help but wonder what's going through her head, but maybe that's something I'm not privy to for a reason.

The drive to Hollyberry Subdivision has a soundtrack: heavy breathing and the occasional staccato of a yawn, the quiet croon of late-night radio, and the buzz of wheels on pavement. As I pull into the Watts' driveway, the curtains rustle and Mrs. Watts' head pokes out in the dimly lit windowpane. She's an excitable woman, and always has been, and I can't say I'm surprised that she waited up to welcome us home.

My phone buzzes in my pocket as I turn off the ignition. A pause, then a second buzz.

"You coming in to say hi to Mom? She's probably going to want all the details of the entire night."

I unbuckle the seatbelt and pull the device from the inside lining of my suit coat, a message from Georgia blinking on the screen.

Georgia: *Dad says okay. Convince Paisley's mom.*

It takes everything in my power not to show any emotion.

"Yeah, of course. Let her know I'm bringing you back home in one piece."

"That's going to be obvious once I walk inside, but thanks for not just dropping me off and driving away like you normally do." She pokes me in the bicep to playfully emphasize her point, just as the front door opens and Mrs. Watts waves at us from the stoop. Paisley opens the door to the Ford Escape, and the bright dome light flashes on, interrupting the allure of the darkness and replacing it with glaring reality.

"You two! You'd be out here talking half the night if I didn't let you know I was still up. How was your night? I bet the school looked beautiful. What did the other girls wear? Did you get your pictures taken at that photo booth you helped organize?"

"Mom, calm down. The night was fine." There's an edge to Paisley's voice that wasn't there before, and it's then and there it hits me that she's actually been stewing all the way home about her mother not letting her go away for one last vacation. "I heard something interesting though. About a trip."

Mrs. Watts turns white.

"Paisley, dear, you have to understand. It's just not safe. Come on inside and we can talk about it some more and I'll explain why your father and I don't think it's a practical idea."

Paisley actually stomps her foot like a child, her shoe hitting the pavement with more force than I anticipated.

"A practical idea? You realize you're talking about my life here? Shouldn't I be the one to decide what I do and don't want to do? How I feel? What I can handle?" Her voice rises with each word, a furious tempest brewing inside of her tiny body. "I'm never going to get to do anything ever again! I barely made it to prom. I don't want coming home from school to be the last trip I ever take. I need to get things done. I need to feel like I'm ready to go."

"Paisley, I—"

It's about time I cut in and say my piece before we wake up the whole neighborhood.

"Actually, Mrs. Watts? Georgia was talking to her father this evening, and he's going to be on the Island for a medical conference the same time we wanted to visit."

There's a pregnant pause, and both women stare at me as if

I've grown three heads. Because of this, I am compelled to keep talking. "We were thinking that maybe if a doctor familiar with Paisley's condition was there with us that maybe you'd consider letting her go. It's obvious it means a lot to her to be able to get all of these things on her bucket list done, and I don't think Georgia will be able to live with herself if this doesn't work out. She's put so much time into working out the details—"

"Mitchell, hush." Paisley holds up one hand, commanding my attention. "Mom, does that change anything?"

Mrs. Watts sighs, wringing her hands.

"I mean, I guess it does mitigate some of the issues your father and I were worried about…" That's all that needs to be said.

Paisley squeals in interrupted excitement out into the tranquility of the subdivision, jumping on me, and wrapping her arms around my neck. For a second I don't know what to do, so I stand there awkwardly as she hugs me and watches Mrs. Watts' expression change from hesitation into happiness. "Now, Paisley, that doesn't mean that there aren't going to be rules."

Paisley releases me and flies over to her mother, embracing her tightly around her thick waist.

"Thank you so much. I can't even tell you how much this means to me."

"Now, you'll need to check in with Georgia's father once a day—"

"Mom, please. We can figure this all out without Mitchell here. I have to be responsible."

Mrs. Watts pats Paisley's arm protectively.

"I just want someone to be able to hold you accountable. I know how vacations get with a bunch of teenagers roaming around unsupervised. I was a kid once too, you know. Now, let's go inside before someone yells out their window at us. We can have a cup of tea before Mitchell heads home for the night. Something to calm us all down."

I don't have the heart to tell her I don't like tea, or that what I really need is one of Dean's cigarettes and a long nap, instead of accepting the offer and walking through the threshold to the Watts' home. Something in Paisley's demeanor has changed - now instead of just being terrified, she's terrified and excited.

EIGHT

~ PAISLEY ~

The morning of graduation, the June sun blasts an unseasonably warm temperature, and I can't help but wonder if I'd be reprimanded for wearing jean shorts to the ceremony instead of my dress.

About a month ago, the school broke it to the grade twelves that there wouldn't be any fancy attire like what we saw on television or in movies. Instead, they would be borrowing the thick black gowns of one of the city universities, and we would wear them instead of tasseled hats and striped collars. Some people were upset to find out they wouldn't get to do the whole ritual with the passing of the hat tassel and all that. But I'll heartily admit, I was relieved that I wouldn't have to worry about yet another piece of awkward clothing, trying to keep the damn thing on my head with my wig in place.

The only downside is I'm wearing a heat absorbing cape of some deadly cotton, and I'm probably going to pass out if Mom and Dad demand any more pictures. He's only been home for a couple of days, but already you'd swear he hadn't left.

The five of us—Mitchell, Taryn, Dean, Georgia, and me—stand in a disheveled line in front of the school marker, an old brick front with a new piece of printed signage in the academic colors of yellow and sapphire. Our parents crouch and lean and prop themselves in front of us in aims of getting a perfect pose, my dad with watering eyes as I hoist myself up on the brick so I can sit. Mitchell leans his arm on Taryn's shoulder, who looks much happier after a day of rest and the permission to wear pants, and she flashes a brilliant smile at the cameras in front of her.

Flash, snap, click.

"Okay." Mom finally breaks up the photo shoot. "Between us all, we've probably got at least one good one. We should head in; the ceremony starts in another few minutes."

Thank God; let's get this over with.

Parents snap covers back on camera lenses as they walk, Dean's mother scrolling through pictures, while his father guides her along the side of the parking lot. Taryn's mother's boyfriend looks rather annoyed that he even has to attend the event, but Taryn hasn't been the easiest person to deal with lately, so maybe they got in another fight this morning. I'd have to ask Georgia if I wanted to know; her proximity gives her details she probably doesn't want in any case.

Within seconds, only Mitchell and I remain, and he offers a hand to help me down from my perch. I take it. Little tendrils of a warm sensation trickle through where he touches me, warming up my arm, and reminding me that I'm harboring something more than friendship. We stand on the lawn as our families and friends pass us, my mother giving me a little wink as if she knows Mitchell and I need the time alone.

"Thank you so much for everything at prom. I've said it a million times, but that really meant a lot to me. And getting my parents to agree to let me go with you guys away? I don't think I'll ever be able to repay you." I cautiously break the ice, tugging a little at the ends of my wig. It's perfectly straight on my head—as always, thanks to glue and careful consideration—but I fidget so much with it sometimes that I don't know how it stays on.

"Payment isn't necessary." Mitchell smiles, finally letting my hand go after holding on to it about ten seconds too long. "Just enjoy yourself."

"Georgia won't even tell me the plans, and she's sworn you all into secrecy. I don't know how she's going to mash everything into one trip. It seems impossible. I mean, some of the things on that list just can't be forced."

I 'm referring to one item, in particular, the one relating to love, and Mitchell's grin breaks my heart into a thousand pieces. I almost get up the courage to tell him that I like him as more than a friend.

Almost.

"Well, you know Georgia. She's always coming up with some kind of scheme," Mitchell offers. "Between the four of us, we'll figure it out."

He shrugs, the fabric of my dress shirt pasting itself onto his skin and reminding me that there's something underneath that cloth other than nakedness.

"You guys coming? We're going to be late," Georgia calls from the front entryway. Her voice shatters the illusion of isolation and brings me back into real time at an alarming rate.

"Come on then," I reply with a little wave to my best friend who shuts the door behind her. "Let's go knock something else off this list of mine before we absolutely decimate it."

My tone is cheery and bubbly, but in reality, I don't want to leave without telling Mitchell that I'm in dire straits. I love him, but I just can't let myself feel that way.

"Are you sure you're dying? I'm not entirely convinced."

I peer down at myself, wiggling the hem of my dress back and forth in the sunlight, little ripples of sharp blue accentuating my pale legs.

"Maybe today I'm not dying, Mitchell. Maybe today I'll be just like everyone else." I turn to head across the grass, the jam-packed parking lot to our left.

Then, a pile of word vomit comes spewing from Mitchell's

mouth as if he's had too much to drink and can no longer control his thoughts.

"You're not everyone else," he tells me, before having the good sense to stop himself, and the seconds suddenly slow to molasses.

"What?" I turn slowly, and my face presumably flushes a gentle rose.

"I mean— I just meant it in the sense that I don't really think of you like I think about other people."

Mitchell, please don't do this.

I walk back to where Mitchell has planted his feet, getting so close to him that the hint of woodsy pine on his skin surrounds me. The voice in my head is telling me to do something that the moment isn't right for, while my hands twitch in unbridled worry. He looks different in this instance, raw and edgy and handsome, like snowy driftwood toiling in the storm of the ocean.

"Mitchell, don't—"

"We're already here, and I'm already saying it, Ley. I can tell by the look in your eyes you feel what I do. Don't discount this. We have time."

"Time, Mitchell?" I laugh, a faint and delicate sound with a boundary of darkness. "I'm on borrowed time. It's the only thing I don't have."

I don't move away as Mitchell's hand makes contact with my arm, and my brain screams a million different directions at me, while my skin sears underneath the ultraviolet rays. He feels it. He felt it at prom, and he feels it now, but I need to admit it to myself before I admit it to him.

I am compulsive in my lack of time.

"I feel it, Mitchell," I say in a small and stammered voice, so tiny I can barely make it out myself. "I've felt it for a while now, but seeing you in that suit for prom—I don't know. It just did something to me. But it's not fair to you. It wouldn't be fair to anyone."

"Why don't you let me decide what's fair and what's not? Wasn't number eight on your list to fall in love?"

"You can be in love with so many things, Mitchell. They don't have to be people. They can be places, ideas, concepts, sounds—"

"Well, I'm in love with the idea of being with you."

Oh, no.

"You'll have to be in love with more than the idea," I note, grasping at straws and reason and logic. "You need to be in love with the reality that someday—a day sooner rather than later—I'm going to die."

"I know," he asserts, slipping his hand down my arm to meet my fingers.

"But do you really? This could never be a normal relationship. This is a fixed timeline of impending disaster all rolled up into a package I don't think you know how to unwrap." I squeeze his fingers in my own before I let them go. I have to get away from him before I do something I regret—something that could tear us apart and change everything we've had for all these years. I get halfway down the sidewalk before Mitchell finally figures out what to say.

"What if I do?" he calls, jogging up behind me, his black cotton gown blowing in the breeze. "What if I do know how to unwrap it? What if you're only saying no because you're scared?"

I whip around, and for a second I consider walloping him across the face to knock some sense into that head of his.

I don't.

"Of course I'm scared, Mitchell! Wouldn't you be scared? One of these days what happened while we were dancing at prom is going to kill me. Do you think I want to die in your arms?" There's a pause, but it's a rhetorical one, space meant for reflection and not for responding. "I don't want to put you through this hell because I see what it's doing to my family. I want to be selfish and try and live with as much normalcy as possible and what would be normal about dating on a deadline? It would be so much easier if I could tell you with absolute certainty that I don't love you. But I do, and that scares me too. Who does this? Who willingly tortures them-selves with the knowledge that someone they love is going to die or that they're going to leave the person they've unknowingly loved for fourteen years?"

Mitchell seems taken aback. He has nothing to say, and so I don't respond either. I'm not really looking for the gratification of my feelings anyway.

"Now, please. Let's just go, graduate, before I croak out here in the parking lot."

In my head I'm cursing at myself, my own devil telling me to kiss him and profess my love for him. On the outside, I remain my scared little self who watches a heartbreak into a million tiny pieces before my very eyes.

NINE

~ MITCHELL ~

I buy a couple of grams of weed from Robbie Marks after the graduation ceremony, my personal contribution to the bonfire that we're going to have on the beach once we get to Partridge Island.

Usually, the others aren't into smoking, but I figure that so many people are using marijuana as therapy now there's no harm in getting Paisley high since she's planning on going off and dying anyway. I hide the little-marked baggies in the back pocket of my dress pants, the wretched things a requirement for the ceremony, along with a half a pack of rolling papers thrown in from Robbie as his own version of a graduation present. Coupled with a bottle of gin I snatched from Dad's liquor cabinet, we're at least off to a good start.

Initially, Georgia had planned for us to take Dean's Mazda over to Partridge Island, but when I brought up the idea of packing luggage and other supplies, she turned the driving over to me and my trusty Ford Escape. The thing is probably as old as the hills, Nolan having driven it over hell and high water in his time living in Hollyberry, but it's been well looked after. On top of that, the inspection is new, so there's only so much we can complain about.

Doctor Hart leaves for Partridge Island two days after graduation, at a time that is much earlier in the morning then I would ever like to be awake in the summer. The only reason I'm aware he's gone is that Georgia texts me and wakes me up, asking if I've printed all of the maps and travel bookings. If nothing else, she's a careful traveler and a determined planner. However, I am thankful that she doesn't propose leaving before noon, because I still have to pack up my things.

By pack, I mean throw some stuff into a bag and leave a goodbye note for the parents so they know not to expect me home for the next few days. I've mentioned the certainty of the trip in passing, but since they're plans with the other four, Mom and Dad don't seem to worry too much about it. Not like Paisley's mother.

But yes, I've printed everything she's asked for.

I pick up Dean last, meaning he doesn't get a choice of seating, mentally making a note to at least try and get him to call the front spot on the way home so the girls can bond in the back.

"How many lectures did you get from Paisley's parents before you were allowed to leave?" Dean asks as he tumbles his way in, crushing my package of smokes on the back seat by accident.

"Oh, about a hundred," Taryn responds with a stifled laugh as Dean tosses his bag over the back divider into the trunk space and buckles his seat belt. "She gave us every medication and every phone number for every pharmacy and hospital and doctor probably on the entire planet. Plus, we had to leave all the contact info for Doctor Hart, and his hotel name and his room number."

"Room 312 at the Rodd by the Conestoga Mall. I don't think I'll ever forget that as long as I live. Then, she cried," Georgia replies, giving me a subtle little wink. "Don't forget that part, Tee. That's important."

Taryn kicks off her flip-flops with an abbreviated chuckle as I turn out of the subdivision onto the main road and pick up speed. Paisley rolls the window of the Escape down a bit farther and makes little waves with her hand in the breeze.

"Don't tell her you saw that. She'll probably be embarrassed for life," Paisley speaks out into the motorized air, and some of the syllables get lost into the atmosphere.

"Speaking of embarrassed for life, we need to get this out now. Dean and Georgia—how long exactly have you guys been sleeping with each other?" Taryn gives them a sly look and I nearly choke on my coffee, Paisley grabbing the cup from my hand and jamming it into the console.

"Couple months," Dean admits, and Georgia punches him in the thigh. "What? Was I supposed to deny it? I mean come on, Taryn lives next door for Christ's sakes. I'm pretty sure she's at least suspected."

A loud laugh rattles in Taryn's throat.

"Suspected, heard, saw. You guys are shit at sneaking around."

I can't tell if Dean is embarrassed or horny at the idea of Taryn seeing him and Georgia getting it on. The look on his face suggests both.

"Then why didn't you just say something?"

Georgia's question comes out more like a lengthy whine, her face a deep red.

"It was way more fun to watch you two squirm at prom when you thought none of us had any idea. Dean, the look on your face when I suggested Mrs. Crocker take a picture of you and Georgia —best moment of my life. It was bound to happen. I mean, statistically."

"Statistically." Georgia groans. "Please, no school talk until September."

Right, September. When she leaves to move halfway across the country, and Dean is stuck here at community college taking welding. He's mentioned his plans before, but now that Georgia is in the picture, his hesitation makes a lot more sense.

"Well then, talk about what you've planned. I want to know!" Paisley twists around in her seat, staring back at the three of them behind her and joining in the banter.

"Nope, not saying anything," Georgia retorts. "And if anyone else blabs with so much as a speck of my premature details then I'm going to throw you into the ocean."

I don't know who she told all of her grand plans to, but it certainly wasn't me.

The drive to Partridge Island is about three hours to the Confederation Bridge, then another forty minutes to Ocean Star Cottages where Georgia's set us up in a chalet for six nights, one of those being Canada Day. The website showed a five bedroom cottage overlooking the Gulf of Saint Lawrence, cedar shingles and weathered roof standing tall on a hill surrounded by a thick red mud driveway and long hayfields. When we get there, it's so much more than I expected, and I have to wonder where Georgia picked up the money to rent this place out for the week. I assume she wrangled all the parents into helping, but as with most things to do with Georgia's schemes, she keeps her sources tight-lipped.

While the girls rush in to take a look around and argue over bedrooms, Dean and I unload the back of the SUV. I don't say much—I have nothing to say, really—but I can't help that I watch over the girls as they prance into the cottage.

"Mitchell? What's going on?"

I jolt back to reality, my daydream is broken into pieces as quickly as it started.

"What do you mean?"

"Don't play that game with me. You're acting like you're lost in this own word of yours. You barely spoke on the way here. Something's rattling around that nerdy head of yours, and you're gonna tell me what it is before the girls come back."

I sigh as I pull Georgia's hot pink gym bag from the trunk and fling it over my shoulder. If there's anyone I should be telling the story of my attraction to Paisley too, it's Dean. We've known each other forever, and the guy has more of my secrets than he probably has of his own.

"I like her, Dean. Like, I really like her. I might love her."

Oh God, the 'L' word. I've used it.

"Who, Taryn? Dude, I hate to break it to you, but I get the feeling she doesn't like you back as more than a friend." I've had the suspicion about Taryn liking girls for a while now, but she's never come out with it, and I don't think it's my place to pry.

"No, I mean Paisley."

"Oh, Mitch. That's even worse. I mean, good for you and all that but——"

"I know what you're going to say. and I've already heard it from Paisley herself." I hike one of two coolers from the Escape, loose ice rattling against the plastic.

"So you told her, hey?"

"I tried. At graduation. Not great timing. But I can't worry too much about timing anymore. The best part of it all is that Paisley told me she's into me too but that it wouldn't be fair to me to try anything."

Dean hauls the other cooler out from the back of the Escape and it thunks onto the red dirt road.

"Ouch. That sucks."

"Tell me about it." I slam the trunk, locking the car doors with a press of the remote. "Now I just feel stupid."

"Give her some space and some time to consider what you've said. That's what I did with Georgia, and she came around. There's something to be said for letting them play the scenario over and over in their head."

"We don't exactly have a lot of time, Dean."

He's right, and he's not all at the same time. I don't know much about women, but I give him the only piece of advice I ever received about girls from my dad.

"No, you're thinking about it all wrong. Pretend you have forever for her."

"Forever?" I laugh. "What about cancer, the migraines, the—I don't know—everything else?"

"Screw everything else, Mitchell. She's the only thing that matters, and if you know you love her then you know I'm right."

There's nothing left for me to say in the matter, a crushed package of smokes and a bottle of scavenged beer calling my name.

TEN

~ PAISLEY ~

Ocean Star Cottage is even more gorgeous than the pictures; a sanctuary down a charming dirt path and overlooking the depth and breadth of the ocean. It takes a second to truly appreciate the architecture of the quaint little building, a curved balcony out front with a barbecue and more deck chairs than we have people. Long seagrass floats toward the foundation, tickling the concrete and swerving in the island breeze. The scents of the beach and sunscreen plants itself firmly on my lips in an offering to taste the first bit of my last summer, and I lick it off and enjoy the way this freedom makes me feel.

The boys hang around outside, less concerned with seeing the space than I am, Georgia and Taryn tear up the drive to stretch their legs from being cramped for the last number of hours. The front door is unlocked, a set of keys immediately on the hook to the inside of the entryway, and salted air blows through the partially opened windows. The chalet's two floors are a country rustic, all exposed beams and patchwork quilts, the kitchen opening into a sunken-in living room complete with stone fireplace, leather couches, and a slate-topped table that probably weighs a ton, and then some.

"Wow, G. This place is amazing," I breathe as Taryn and Georgia break into the kitchen bar where the owners have left a case of raspberry cordial on the counter—a welcome gift from the Island. Georgia pops the lid off a bottle with a snap against the granite countertop, handing it across the surface to me before taking care of another for Taryn.

"I'd say. Do I even want to know how much this cost?" Taryn takes a drink of her pink liquid, drowning herself in half the bottle before coming up for air.

"You don't. You can thank my dad later. You'll both be glad to know that he was fully supportive of our little bucket list adventure. I just had to promise him we were all going to sleep in separate beds."

Taryn mumbles something as she tries to swallow a mouthful of liquid. "Speaking of beds, we should pick out our bedrooms before the boys get in here and take the best ones. I'm not giving up a queen sized bed to Mitchell who I guarantee isn't even going to use it. He'll probably be up most nights with his laptop playing games online."

Georgia giggles, taking a drink from her glass bottle, peeling at the yellow label.

"I saw the room I want online," she notes. "It's at the back with the big picture of the fox above the headboard. I fully anticipate breaking my promise to my father about the whole bed agreement, and I'm happy to situate myself as far away from you all as possible."

Taryn pretends to gag on her cordial, and I turn red at Georgia's blatant admission.

"Well, I'm taking a room upstairs then," Taryn notes as she places her bottle on the counter next to the kitchen sink. "I'll be leaving the worst of the rooms for the boys. Paisley, you want to come with?"

"Sure, but I want to poke around down here a little in case

there's a cute bedroom I don't want to miss. This whole place has so much character."

"What, you mean like this one?" Taryn points toward a door stuck halfway underneath the staircase, one corner cut off at the edge to make the entryway fit without compromising the molding. There's a little tin star nailed to the wood; something makes it seem charming and also cozy.

At first, I can't tell if the space is meant to be a sleeping area, but once I poke my head in, there's just enough room for one single bed and a big floor length window overlooking the field. The early evening sun crests the hill and shines on a tall antique bureau, a little glass collection of candles glowing with battery operated flames. A knitted blue rug coils across the hardwood and matches the sky coloring of the walls.

I could live in this room forever.

"Cute space, Ley. You claiming this room?" Taryn peers in, leaning on the crooked frame with a new drink in her hand.

I drop myself on the wrought iron bed, a memory foam mattress soft underneath me.

"Definitely. I love the light in here. But I want to see the others before the guys mess them all up."

"Well, then we'd better hurry because they're dragging stuff in as we speak."

As if on cue, there's a crash in the living room, and I fly off the bed—the sound of every one of our bags bring dropped at the same time. I half curse in my head at Mitchell and Dean, though my other half thanks them because at least I didn't have to haul everything in.

"All right, everyone finds their own shit. I'll take whatever room's left because I don't plan on sleeping. There's a beer in that cooler with my name on it, and I'm going to drink it on the patio." Mitchell winks at me, flipping up the top of the ice box and digging around inside. "Crazy door belongs to you, hey? I'll try and remember that another ten beers from now. At least you're at the bottom of the steps."

"Don't be disgusting," I scoff, doing my best impression of someone who doesn't like the teasing. I'm surprised at the rash nature of his comment, but nobody else is paying attention to us at all.

Dean hands Georgia a beer, popping off the top on the edge of the counter before slamming the screen door behind him. I don't know how both of them manage to open bottles this way without cracking the glass, but something tells me that they've been performing this party trick for longer than I ever could have guessed.

"I have to hand it to you, Georgia. He's not a bad catch. I mean, there were worse guys in school than Dean. I won't deny that it's a little weird knowing that you've seen his… man parts." I punctuate my attempt at a joke with a swig of the end of my cordial, replacing the bottle in my hand with an opened beer from the counter.

Taryn chokes on her drink.

"God, please warn me before you say things like that. I need time to prepare myself for the mental image of Georgia and Dean getting it on."

"You're not supposed to picture it, Tee," Georgia notes dryly. "But to be fair, you know, Mitchell's a pretty good catch too. I don't think you should discount him, Ley. Especially not after prom."

I take a swig of the chilled beer, a small piece of ice sliding off the bottle and hitting the floor.

"Yeah, the problem is that I'm dying, and I can think of about a million other girls who deserve someone like that more than I do." I shrug as if her comments mean absolutely nothing and if my feelings aren't things that matter anymore.

"Wait, hold up." Taryn gulps the last of her second drink and plops the empty glass on the countertop. The girl sure can put away a load. "What's going on with Mitchell?"

I sigh, a shy little smile breaking out on my face as I recall the conversation.

"He told me he likes me. At graduation. I told him to forget about it. I feel bad, but what else am I supposed to do?"

"Anything! Literally, anything you want, Ley! You're the one that keeps talking about using all your last moments up and crap. It's not like Mitchell doesn't know you're dying. Hell, we all know it all too well. If he still wants it, I say give it."

I suck back a bigger mouthful of beer than I probably should, nearly choking on the liquid. This forces me to punctuate my statement with an awkward cough, just as Dean slams the screen door.

"Here's the rest of the food. Mitchell's already retired. I want whatever bedroom has the biggest bed." Dean winks, and Georgia scowls.

"You can sleep on the lawn?" Taryn smiles, popping the cap off another beer.

"You'd better slow down, Taryn, or you'll be the one on the lawn. Now if you ladies will excuse me, I'm taking this beer and one of Mitchell's cigarettes, and I'm going to start my vacation. But before I forget," Dean adds as he pulls a sheet of paper from his pocket, "here's our to-do list. I've already taken the liberty of marking off a couple of things."

He snaps the page to the fridge with a magnet shaped like a lighthouse.

"I'll be leaving the rest of the items up to Georgia because she's the only organized person out of this whole group." Dean drops a little kiss to the side of her head, and she swats him away playfully as if she's still playing the game where we all pretend not to know about their relationship.

"Okay, so I guess since we've all made it here we can mark off number four: go on a friend vacation. We officially did that." Georgia scrounges up a pen from the countertop and puts a squiggly line through the scrawled handwriting as Dean slams the screen door.

"G, this doesn't have to all be planned." I poke my head over her shoulder. "Let's just have a good week. It means a ton that you did this for me. But right now I want to find my bedroom, see what the boys broke in my bag, and have some dinner. Everything else can come later."

Georgia takes a deep breath, trying to relax her Type A personality.

"Okay. Sounds good." She smiles, and it becomes evident that my permission was just the thing she needed.

Back behind the kitchen is another bedroom, secluded from the rest of the cottage and separated with a bathroom. Both Taryn and I are a little bit jealous that the room has an en-suite, but wordlessly agree that Georgia should get the space as her own for the week as she requested. Much like me, she doesn't even want to see the other rooms; she's in love with the lace pillows and knitted throw on the bed, a big picture of a fox on the farthest wall like what she described from the online photographs.

The bedrooms upstairs have equal charm, Taryn picking the one to the end of the hall with a balcony overlooking the side field. She drags her stuff into the space and plunks it on the bed as Georgia, and I wrangle Mitchell and Dean's packs and deposit them in the other two rooms to get them out of the way. By the time we get back to the kitchen after making an executive decision about which boy got what room—Dean in the middle and Mitchell at the top of the steps—Taryn's seasoning thawed burgers with some orange colored spice, dipping into the coolers to find her supplies.

"Dean's got the barbecue going. I'm starving. I took out all the boxed meat so I hope you're hungry."

A half-hour later, about the time when the fake cheese slices come out, hunger hits me like a brick wall. The five of us sit on the patio in the fading summer light as if nothing is wrong, and we've just come out to this cottage to celebrate the end of the school year and the start of our new semi-adult lives. As I shove burger after burger in my mouth, I witness little explosions between Dean and Georgia, the two of them feeling some sense of relief at finally being able to show their real emotions, and Taryn is only half paying attention to her food between text messages. Mitchell and I share these stolen glances with one another through the course of dinner, unspoken questions floating from one side of the table to the other and back again. Maybe we would be like Dean and Georgia if we gave ourselves a chance at being something.

We must sit out on the porch for a few hours, at least, the conversation flowing every way imaginable until the light fades and the bottles pile up. Mitchell pulls out a bag of weed, and he lets me roll a joint to pass around, just enough of a high going between us that we finally realize we're all alone here in this field and we're a long way from home. Taryn uses the barbecue lighter to set flame to some citronella torches at the corners of the deck, the lemon smoke shooing away the early evening insects. At the edge of the grass, there are a couple of foxes that bound by, chasing a field mouse or a discarded hamburger or anything else they can scavenge before the day fades away. Dean holds Georgia's fingers in his under the hem of the wooden table and then realizes that they don't have to be secretive anymore, so he places them on his lap.

The candles dwindle, as they do when time passes, and soon Taryn heads to bed, and we find ourselves paired off in conversations.

"Hey, look. There's the Big Dipper." Mitchell points toward the midnight blue, frogs peeping in the distance. I crane my neck backward to stare at where his finger is trying to show me, but all that appears up there are the dots of millions of stars that don't seem to make a picture at all. "It kind of looks like a pot; four stars in a square with a handle."

"I don't see it," I admit after a few moments pass. Everything up there looks like a dark mass of tiny bits of light, not a pot or a handle or whatever a dipper is supposed to look like.

"Hang on; I have an idea." Mitchell pulls his phone from his pocket and taps on the screen a few times before flipping the device over to me. The front is black, nothing appearing. "Turn it up toward the sky. I've got this app called Starry Night. It's a neat little program that shows you where all the constellations are based on your geographical location."

I tip the device, so the camera is facing toward the moon, and to my delight, a moon appears on the Starry Night screen with a label, along with scattered lines showing other celestial pictures— Cygnus, Draco, Cassiopeia.

"Hey, this is pretty cool." I hold the phone up over my face and spin it in a slow half-circle around my chair to see what other images appear.

"If you find a constellation, you can just click on it, and the app will give you the story behind the name. You can even save all the ones you spot to a profile. Everything has a label attached to it, even individual stars."

"Why do you have this?" I don't break my gaze from the screen as I ask the question, Ursa Minor slowly coming into view as I shift the phone's camera back and forth. "It seems so random. I mean, it's cool, but how did you even find this?"

"I don't know, really," Mitchell replies. "Found it in my internet travels, I guess. Just seemed like something you might enjoy."

I twirl back around to the moon again before dropping my gaze back to Mitchell. Dean and Georgia are speaking in hushed tones around us, leaning forward on their elbows with their faces nearly touching as they converse.

"Do you think they want some time alone?" I ask Mitchell, tilting my head over to one side. "Maybe we should head to bed and let them process everything that's happened today. It was kind of a big deal for them to let us all know the truth about what's going on between them.

"If we both leave at the same time, I bet they'll start thinking the same thing about us," he says with a wink. "You get some sleep. I'll be in shortly. Apparently, there's supposed to be some space junk floating by soon, and I'm curious if the app will pick it up."

"Okay. Good night then."

"Night, Songbird."

Stifling a yawn, I grab the remainder of my bottle of beer and bring it inside with me, walking along the backlit cottage windows and opening the screen door with a muted squeal. I am careful not to let the door slam in case Taryn is already asleep, though I suspect she's up in bed texting whoever it is that's been keeping her interest this whole trip so far. Inside is quiet, the floor creaking as I step across it, my footing not all that steady considering the amount of weed I've smoked. Nevertheless, I make it to my bedroom under the stairs, closing myself in the pastel walls while fake candle flames sparkle along the window.

I'm tired, but I'm not that tired, and so I make to unpack a few of my things, figuring I'll make proper use of some of the beautiful furniture and move in for the week. I set the beer bottle down on the bureau top and rummage through my bag, lifting it onto the mattress, and pulling out a collection of hoodies, tank tops, and the bottles of medicine that my mother forced me to pack. The orange containers get shoved to the bottom of my bag while the sweaters are moved to the dresser drawers; once I open the first one, I find that it is filled with books. Many of them are titles I don't recognize, but there's an ancient copy of *The Virgin Suicides* stuck in the corner, pages all dog-eared and well-loved. By the time I finish drinking and flicking through the pages, I assume the others have been knocked unconscious by fatigue and sunshine rather than the liquor and drugs. The cottage is still and thick with silence.

The moon sits low in the sky, indicating the time of night, and wordlessly suggesting that I should get some sleep.

I slip out of my jean shorts and toss them on the bedside chair, crawling in between the cascade of pillows and clean sheets with my wig still on my head. The covers smell like a combination of clean laundry and Christmas trees, and I suck the scent in because it reminds me of home. Also, as I roll over, I see all the stars quite clearly through the floor-length glass, and for a second I think about if Mitchell found his space junk all the way out in the universe.

Paisley: *It's so quiet in here. Did you find your space garbage?*

I type out the text message quickly, my fingers slipping over the screen of the phone a couple of times before I'm able to get the words out correctly. Mitchell might not even be awake anymore.

Mitchell: *Helps me think. And no, maybe I had the wrong night.*

Paisley: *What are you thinking about?*

Mitchell: *Everything, and nothing.*

That seems like quite the loaded response, but I'm not sure if it's a hint for me to keep talking or a clue for me to shut up and mind my own business.

Paisley: *That's a lot to have going on.*

Mitchell: *Remember our conversation at grad? I can't stop thinking about it. And I can't sleep.*

My heart somersaults in my throat as I tap back another message with a massive smile across my face.

Paisley: *Neither can I. Want to go for a walk? Maybe we will see that space garbage after all.*

I roll over onto my back, the phone above my face, waiting for a response. Thirty seconds go by, then a minute. I'm at the point of wondering if Mitchell fell asleep on me when there's a soft rapping on the door that makes me half jump out of my skin. Throwing off the covers, I pad halfway to the door before I remember I hopped into bed in my underwear, and this might not be the best way to go out walking in the middle of the night. My jean shorts have slipped to the floor off the chair, and I pull them on just a moment before the knocking happens again—a little louder this time.

"Hey," I whisper as I open the door. "I'm just going to grab a sweater; then we can go."

"You say that like it's the arctic out there. It's got to be still twenty-five Celsius." Mitchell is still fully dressed from dinner, and I only assume he was up in his room playing a game on his phone before I started texting him.

"I'm more worried about the bugs. The last thing I need is to be covered in a bunch of bites. You want to see me be miserable?" I joke with the last part, reaching over to the dresser to fetch a pink hoodie from the top of the bureau. As I do so, I knock my discarded and empty beer bottle to the floor with a crash. It doesn't smash, thank God, but it makes enough of a racket that I'm sure everyone in the house is awake if they weren't before.

Mitchell and I stand there in the doorway stock still, waiting for the sounds of someone stirring, but the noise doesn't come. The only thing we can hear is the hum of the refrigerator running across the hallway in the kitchen, and the tick-tick-tick of the hallway clock keeping time.

"You're going to give someone a heart attack, Songbird." Mitchell's face is red in the candlelight, shadows from our bodies being cast down the hardwood. "Come on, let's get out of here before you break something else and we start rumors."

I close the bedroom door behind us with a little click, mainly so that if anyone happens to walk by they'll think I'm asleep and not out traipsing around in the dark with Mitchell. He leads me through the dimly lit corridor past the kitchen, grabbing an unopened bottle of red wine and a corkscrew from the counter as we amble past.

"We need sustenance, of course," he whispers.

"That usually refers to food," I reply with a stifled giggle. "But in this case, we can make an exception."

The air outside is just as warm as Mitchell had advised, but I put on my sweater anyway to keep the cool undertones of the night air from prickling my skin. He sets the wine on the patio table before popping the cork with little effort, handing me over the bottle to take the first drink. The liquid feels smooth on my throat, the taste is more like raspberries than whatever Taryn was sharing with me earlier while we were smoking.

"So," Mitchell states, accepting the wine back and taking a long drink. "Tell me about why you couldn't sleep."

"I was about to ask you the same question, actually," I admit. "It seems like you probably have more to say on the topic than I do."

Mitchell sighs audibly, taking another swig from the bottle.

"It's nothing, really. Just, promise me that you'll think about what I said."

I don't tell him that I haven't stopped thinking about it, or him, for a very long time.

"I promise. You say that like I have some aversion to you, Mitchell. I don't. What I have is an aversion to hurting you." Leaning against the balcony railing, an owl hoots from over in the eastward trees. The sound is lonely and solitary.

"Don't you think I should be the one to decide what's going to hurt me and what won't?" He offers over the wine to me but I don't drink from it right away, instead holding it in my hand and feeling the weight of the liquid. His voice is slurred just enough that I'm able to notice. How many of these words he would be saying if he didn't have the courage that came from the bottom of a bottle?

"Well?"

"Yes... I mean, I think so," I stutter, placing the carafe down on the porch table. "But this isn't just about you. This is about me too."

Mitchell turns to face me, his eyes stony and serious but his demeanor soft.

"Remember I asked you earlier if you felt it? The feeling between us that is," he clarifies.

"Of course I do. It's been there for a while. I don't know why it's becoming more of a thing now but maybe the lack of time we have actually to do something about it has put a little pressure on us, to be honest."

"If we're being honest, I have to tell you that I feel it all the time when I'm with you. I've felt it in the Escape, at dinner, at prom. It was there when I watched you walk across the stage at graduation." Mitchell takes a step forward, tentatively, as if he is trying his hardest to be brave and do something entirely out of his comfort zone. "And I feel it now."

He brushes one hand up my arm, his touch radiating through the fabric of my sweater and sinking deep into my pores. I can't help but watch his fingers sweep their way up to my neck, the motion carefully calculated with only a bit of nervous tension behind it. There's a little tingling feeling where our skin touches, and this kind of reaction has never happened to me before.

"Mitchell—" I start to speak, but the sound of the screen door slamming throws me backward.

"Am I interrupting something?" Taryn's voice cuts through the moment like a knife.

"Not at all." Mitchell clears his throat and leans back over the railing, picking up the bottle of wine. "We just couldn't sleep. Nothing helps a wandering mind like the night air."

"And a little wine?" She chuckles, giving me a look.

"Wine solves everything." I shrug with a smile.

"Hand it over then, because I'm tired of listening to Georgia and Dean having sex in the room next to mine. At least if I'm drunk, I can attempt to block out Georgia's half-assed attempts at being quiet."

A little peek of sunshine appears over the horizon as we stand on the patio, sharing sips of liquor until the bottle has been drained, which doesn't take much time. I'm the first to start yawning again, my eyes growing heavy and my brain starting to turn off and make passes toward sleeping slowly. I'm a half a second away from turning in for the night—or morning, I suppose —when Mitchell points up at a nearly unidentifiable lump in the sky.

"I guess I did have the date right." He pulls out his phone from his shorts pocket and pokes at the screen. He's opening up Starry Night. "Look, there's my space junk."

"Little smaller than I would have expected," Taryn teases, and I hold back laughter as I watch the little blob of space hurtle through the galaxy and disappear.

ELEVEN

~ PAISLEY ~

When I wake up a few hours later, a pounding has taken hold in my head, a deep and tympanic rhythm in my skull that is lessened only by the consistent shoveling of pieces of fruit into my mouth.

I'm the first one of the morning to discover that the owners of Ocean Star Cottage were nice enough to leave us with an over-flowing basket of real sustenance in the fridge—oranges, cheese, apples, kiwi fruits and a pineapple—maybe as a hint that we should remember to eat something worthwhile. After last night and the wine and the pain radiating over half my body, they might have had the right idea.

Despite my residual headache, it's clear Dean's in the shower with Georgia for a few reasons. One, his cigarettes are on the hallway table just outside the door. Two, my subconscious is flaring up with an abnormally jealous tendency that they are permitted to have a normal relationship while I'm being denied the capacity. Three, and most obviously, I wasn't born yesterday and, the two of them are making a hell of a lot of noise. However, contrary to my expectations, the sounds coming from behind the door aren't ones of muffled passion, but rather words of emotional contemplation and silent breaking points. I recall Georgia and Dean sat outside for a while last night, and it seems to me the conversation may have turned serious after the rest of us fell into bed for the night but before we bothered getting up again.

My intuition prickles as I step away, but the sensation fizzles out quickly. Maybe that's the part of my brain the cancer's eating up for a late breakfast, chewing away the morsels as I try to use them. I stick a slice of orange in my mouth, kind of an homage to what was my cerebellum, and slam the screen door to meet Taryn outside.

It takes another fifteen minutes for Georgia and Dean to appear by Mitchell's Escape looking a little out of sorts. The sun is bright and hot, a perfect Canada Day, with the temperature pushing thirty Celsius and the humidity at a tolerable level. Bits of sea spray float on the airwaves as Taryn and I sit on the veranda steps looking at pictures on her photo account, scrolling over colored squares. It's almost as if she's let me in on some secret part of her life, an intimate section of her very being that she's only sharing with me because I have the convenient future of keeping permanent secrets.

"You guys ready?" Georgia's hair piles on her head in a wet bun, rays of light scintillating hues of auburn and violet on the strands. She's wearing a cute striped tank top with a big pineapple captured on the front; oversized sunglasses clipped to the low neckline. Something about her always looks elegant, in the same way that something about me always looks like I'm ready to kick it. I falter along the lines of persistent mortality.

Nobody waits for a response before piling into the SUV, Dean claiming the shotgun seat and leaving us girls to squander over the air conditioning in the back.

I mentally kick myself for not bringing another orange.

The drive to the Cavendish Boardwalk Shops takes about a half an hour, give or take, just long enough for my right arm to burn through the window glass under the intensified sunlight. The trip is noisy, between Mitchell's music and everyone's voices, but instead of participating I watch the trees and red fields roll by, waving my wiggling fingers at the milk cows in their mottled glory. By the time we find a parking spot in the packed gravel lot however long later, my skin is red and hot to touch, a sensation of nausea hitting me every time I poke at it. I should have put sunscreen on, but it's a little too late for that though—not that I need to worry about skin cancer. A perk for dying already, I suppose.

As I writhe my way out of the cramped back seat, another wave of sickness washes over me, and I start to grow foggy.

"Where should we go first, Ley?" Mitchell hits the automatic lock on the Escape, and the five of us stand in our semi-secluded spot by the trunk. His voice rustles me into awareness, and I jump without realizing I'm doing it, stuck latently in my own little world where I'm preoccupied with my internal battle. I rub my burnt arm, small webs of flaming red appearing like a flag of distraction. The feeling almost makes the nausea go away.

Almost.

"Might as well start on one end and walk our way over to the tattoo place on the other side." Georgia suggests before I have a chance. It's just as well because if I open my mouth other than to breathe, I'm going to puke all over the parking lot.

"Sounds good to me," Dean agrees, slipping one of his hands firmly into Georgia's grasp. Taryn gives me a little wink as she charges ahead to lead the way, phone in one hand and sending a message without as much as a glance down.

I want to follow them, but feet are made of cement, and I stick to the spot.

Mitchell stands across from me with a knit brow as our friends' footsteps crunch away. Ahead, Taryn, Dean, and Georgia dissipate into the generic sounds of an outdoor crowd, ambling along the boundary of the unpaved drive. Taryn's head blends into a collection of teen girls at the door of a shop, and then Georgia and Dean are gone too, somewhere past a line of bins.

"Are you okay?" Mitchell sounds worried. I hate worrying him. I nod, or at least I try to, the up and down motion of my head making me half-seasick.

"Mhmm."

Mitchell isn't buying it, but I can't tell to what degree because I'm trying so hard to keep my stomach in the right spot while my eyes blur with hot tears.

"Hey, talk to me."

He puts his hand on my unscathed arm but I just can't. His skin touching mine makes me anxious, and the anxiety on top of the queasy feeling inside my ribcage is uncomfortable at best.

I panic, and I don't know what to do. I'm going to get sick right here in front of Mitchell on Canada Day when we're supposed to be having a party for me, the goddamn death queen of Partridge Island.

"Ley?"

I ignore Mitchell, and the feeling boils, rolling like a pot of water ready for cooking. I try to force it to simmer, but it doesn't work, steaming from underneath the lid. My insides coil up, knotted, making me light-headed. Then there's a slow buzzing in my ears that negates all of Mitchell—his voice, his atmosphere, his aura—and there is nothing left but a primal flight instinct. So I flee, collapsing behind the Escape, noisily throwing up the breakfast tangerines I ate for brunch.

It's embarrassing.

I don't know how long it takes before I stop dry heaving. It could be seconds, minutes, hours, days, but by that time the grass is littered with satsuma colored pulp and stomach acid that will probably burn a hole through to the center of the universe. Out of the corner of my eye, I spot Mitchell sitting on the back bumper of the Escape, calm contemplation written on his face, a handful of wet wipes in one hand and a bottle of water in the other.

"Here," he says in a gentle voice as I fall back against the trunk door. I take a couple of the moist towelettes from between his fingers and rub at my face, carefully wiping the creases of my lips and down my chin. "Drink this. Slowly, or you'll make yourself sick again."

Crushing the damp cloths in my fist, I grasp the water bottle and slurp at the mouth as delicately as I can muster.

"I'm sorry."

"What for?" Mitchell takes the wipes from me and dumps them in a bin one car down. I take another sip of the warm water, feeling it slosh in my empty stomach.

"I'm a disaster."

"You're sick."

So I am.

I wobble some water around in between my cheeks and spit it onto the gravel, repeating the action a couple of times. Mitchell watches my movements, likely carefully calculating the moment he should telephone Georgia's father and have him drag me into emergency. But there's another look in his eyes, one I recognize from when I fell out of the old maple tree in his front yard.

He cares. What a damn waste of his resources.

"Why do you even want to be a part of this willingly?" I whisper, punctuating the question with another dribble of water.

He gives me a sideways glance as if scoffing at my question that he's already answered a million times before.

"Really?"

I cap the bottle, staring him dead in the eyes.

"Really, Mitchell?"

He reaches over and tugs my wig to one side, straightening it out on my head.

"Because I adore you. I've spent most of my life adoring you, and I want to spend the rest of your life in a state of mutual adoration."

I chuckle, a warm flush crawling up my neck as I dig out some gum from my bag. "You just watched me puke behind your car."

He doesn't miss a beat.

"I'd do it again if you'll let me."

I throw the water bottle at him and bounce off the bumper, my stomach having settled. Taryn, Georgia, and Dean are probably wondering what happened to us.

"You're warped, Mitchell."

He grabs my hand and pulls me down onto his lap, and I squeal before I consider it's a stupid reaction to have. My vision goes blurry for a second, the abruptness of the action throwing my brain off balance.

"Like I said, I adore you, Paisley Watts."

The words run like rivers from his mouth, slow and rocky, with our lips so close together I get the undertone of spearmint and one of Dean's leftover cigarettes. On top, the dusky woods of Mitchell's soap and the crisp scent of shower water trickles into my nose while the taste of the midday heat is running up my legs. If this were a movie, we'd probably kiss right now. Then again, if my life were a movie, it would be a sad excuse for a storyline.

I sigh and stand, our fingers intertwined. Mitchell concedes.

"I'll convince you yet," he smiles.

He's already convinced me, but I can't tell if I want to let him know that or not.

TWELVE

~ MITCHELL ~

Paisley hurts my head and my heart, simultaneously, and separately.

It makes me want a beer and another one of Dean's cigarettes. I'm not a smoker, not even close or by any stretch, but there's something about emotions that get me into vices. It's a funny thing, the way she's able to do that, unlike any of the other prep girls at school even though they tried so hard. They seem so far away now, days into eternities; I suppose there's a lot to be said for history and time and space and everything in between.

With our fingers still laced together, Paisley and I meander along the graveled path in a semi-satisfied silence. The ground crunches under my shoes and her espadrilles, a squashing rhythm of pebbles as we secretly glance at each other and pretend we don't meet eyes. We catch up to Taryn, Dean, and Georgia on the edge of the boardwalk, shuffling in with the crowd as if we hadn't been left behind. Dean's messy hair carries above an outdoor rack of sweaters, his height giving his position away while the girls are huddled in Ocean Surf Shop perusing a wall full of flip-flops in every color under the rainbow. Georgia must have at least five pairs tucked under her arm, stuffing more into the crevice as we approach.

"You sure you're okay?" I have to ask even though the question gives me the sensation of being Paisley's babysitter. Thankfully she only nods and flashes me a sweet smile, one that crumples up my insides as her fingers draw from my own, and she takes the scent of her jasmine perfume with her.

The lemon yellow sunlight streaks through the fake window-panes of the temporary hut, making shuttered lines on the click-down floor. A light breeze bristles the reeds at the edge of the roof and the ends of Paisley's black wig, causing little strands of both to be displaced in the Island air. Around us, music plays from a set of speakers behind the cash register—something vaguely punk rock, from the early 2000's.

"I'm fine. It's kind of like morning sickness, but without the baby." Paisley shrugs.

"So, not like morning sickness at all?"

She runs one hand along my bare arm, bristling the hairs with her touch. It's a simple action, one that an outsider probably wouldn't give a second thought to, but I do. There's something underlying in that connection, a closeness, and it makes my heart do cartwheels in my chest.

"Please stop worrying, Mitchell. We need to have fun. *You* need to have fun and relax." She puts particular emphasis on the part of the sentence referring to me. "Let's buy some shit we don't need with the money we saved for university and get temporary tattoos like badasses from the mainland."

When she says it, it doesn't sound like such a bad idea.

"Paisley! The sandals are buy one get one free! I need one more pair." Georgia waves from across the store, beckoning her over.

Paisley runs a hand through the hair of her wig, a movement that makes it almost seem like her own.

"I've got this. I'll let you know the second I don't. Promise."

I hesitate, but I have to trust her. "Okay."

Paisley scrambles between shelves and racks to join up with Georgia and Taryn, leaving me alone in the center of the surf shop.

I'm not really alone, per se, at least forty other people are crammed in and browsing. The two blonde girls behind the cash register are processing purchases as fast as their fingers can punch the screens of their payment devices, matching ponytails bobbing.

I'm not much in the mood to buy anything, so I stand out on the veranda with Dean, leaning over the edge of the railing.

"Where'd you two mosey off to?" Dean blows out a mouthful of acrid smoke, little curlicues of grey amidst the bright atmosphere.

"Paisley's sick. Well, she was sick. There was some puking happening. Don't tell her I told you."

He nods.

"She okay now?" Dean flips the cigarette over to me but I wave it away.

"Says she's fine. I don't know."

A hum escapes his lips as he sucks away at the burning stick, pushing a chunk of hair out of his face with his free hand. My mother always says that Dean's hair reminds her of a sheepdog, but he insists there's a classic quality to his coiffed style; old-fashioned and matching his jeans, suspenders, and open white dress shirt. A little bit of him could be from a great early American classic, while the other parts are jammed together from the age of jazz and prohibition.

"She'll tell you if something's really wrong, you know that," Dean offers, snubbing out the last drag of his cigarette on the unpainted beam of the patio. He rests his shoulder against the wood, staring off into the inside of the surf shop as the girls stand in line. "You guys have something. You're trying to deny it, but it's been there since we were kids. You always protected her, Mitchell."

He's right. I hate that he's right.

The Boardwalk takes us at least three hours to peruse, shops filled with handicrafts and souvenir shirts and soap made of seaweed packed against the corridors in brightly colored strips. Bustles of tourists clamor around us, shifting fabrics on racks or eating ice cream under wooden awnings and on blankets placed on grassy knolls. We each pick up a few little things, save for Georgia who goes a bit over the top in the spending department, and find ourselves heading to the tattoo and face painting shack near a quarter to four. The sun has retreated into a low blaze over the trees, starting a slow descent into the waters of the Avalon Gulf.

"I need to sit, please." Georgia groans, her feet and shoulders red and burnt from the afternoon. Taryn's neck is the color of an angry cooked lobster; the two of them almost match in skin tone despite their ethnicities. "I have aloe in the car and water. I'm not going to make it to mini golf or a bonfire if I don't get to sit down."

"Why don't you guys go to the car and Mitchell and I will go to the tattoo place? It's not going to be that long. Then whatever I get is a surprise," Paisley shrugs, motioning for the keys to the Escape. I pull them from my pocket, handing them to her without a second thought, and she tosses them to Dean.

"I'm about ready for another smoke," he admits. "We'll see you guys in a few."

We split unevenly, Taryn, Georgia, and Dean heading down the steps to the parking lot, while Paisley and I turn the corner of the strip. A light, late afternoon breeze picks up, cooling the air but not the tension between us. Luckily there's a break in the crowd, and the partition with the shop she's heading for is almost entirely silent.

Paisley walks up to the large picture window where an assortment of designs are stuck, worn sheets of white paper displaying maybe fifty or so options. I spot a little boy, maybe three or four, with his father in the converted cottage. A guy around my brother Nolan's age is henna stenciling the kid's bicep in an electric blue pile of flames, little bits of laughter tinkling out the open door. His hair is the same raven color as Paisley's wig.

"What are you thinking about getting?" I ask as she leans toward the glass. Her face has the soft and rosy glow of someone who forgot to put on an extra coat of sunscreen as the day wore on and the lotion wore off. Underneath the highlights on her cheeks, she looks exhausted and thin. If only there was a more definitive way to know when she was going to go. I'd ask a psychic if I knew one—and if I believed in that sort of thing.

"I kind of like the henna mandalas. A round one on top of my hand so I can look at it when I'm feeling like ditching my list."

"Like earlier when you were puking in the parking lot?"

I have absolutely no class sometimes, but she smiles at me and that makes up for my stupidity.

"Yes, like that."

We stand there, all gathered around, perusing the taped-up drawings and brushing up against each other carefully. We're both too scared to make a move, too worried about each other's rejection, limitations, or comprehension of the implications of our actions. My fingers graze her elbow, once, and her hand trails along my back as she passes behind me to absently stare at another collection of selectable designs. I almost say something, but then the little coal-haired boy gallops out the doorway and interrupts my moment.

"Look, lady! I'm on fire!" His sneakers clap against the wood as he prances in a sing-song voice along the corridor, his father and an oversized shopping bag in tow.

Paisley laughs the way my mother laughs at the antics of a child, and reality smashes me in the face with the reminder that she'll never get to be a mom. It's unfortunate because she'd be a wonderful one.

The man from the shop leans against the door frame, his buzzed blond head and plaid farm shirt giving him two different looks all in one. An intricate floral tattoo, a real one, curls up his forearm, while other little henna designs dot the empty spaces in between.

"Got time for one more if you're interested. Though you two look about old enough for a real tattoo. I do those too, just summer's better for the henna business with all the families kicking about. I'm Adam, by the way."

"Paisley," she notes. "And Mitchell."

Adam shakes my hand like a proper country man would. Once we break, Paisley brushes her fingers along the man's arm, examining his ink with no regard for personal space.

"This is gorgeous," she breathes, turning his arm over in her tiny hands. "I like this little flower here the best."

She's pointing to a little bundle of delicate blue flowers with yellow middles.

"Those are forget me nots." Adam smiles. "I'll be able to free-hand those on to you in probably fifteen minutes. Cute little guys. They'd really suit you. Maybe on your left wrist? Here?"

He flips her hand over and exposes the blue underside veins of her arm, the skin pale and vanilla against his tanned self.

Paisley nods, slipping the fingers of her other hand between my own and squeezing.

"Okay," she replies in a small voice, her hesitation showing through both on her face and through the pressure with which she crushes my fingers. "I just—I'm nervous. Is it normal to be nervous?"

Adam smiles, his bright white teeth showing a little gap.

"Absolutely. But I'm sure you've gone through worse before in your life," he notes, not knowing how accurate his statement is. "Something small like this on your wrist shouldn't cause too much pain. I always describe it as a cat scratch—over and over. Some people hardly notice, others find it a little itchy and annoying. Just know we can take as many breaks as you want. I'm not going anywhere important tonight."

Paisley gives me this sweet and anxious grin.

"Alright. I'm in. Who knows, maybe I'll be back tomorrow for another one. Maybe I'll turn my whole body into a canvas."

We step into the shop, photographs of children with henna paint on their faces and arms lining one wall, interspersed with snapshots of adults with tattoos of varying sizes and complexities. Adam strolls across the entryway, leading us to a bright back room, past a lineup of chairs and a collection of decorative plants. The space is small but well-appointed, little bits of Island life found all around—from the window sills to the collection of sea glass in a fishbowl on one side table.

"This is so pretty," Paisley notes, eyeing the jar and pulling out a chunk of pink glass shaped like a diamond. "I hear rose pieces are rare, especially this size."

"I found that one while I was out surfing. Bailed off my board and ended up under a big wave." Adam wipes off a table and gestures for Paisley to hop up on it. "I was in a relatively shallow area but there was a storm coming and it swept up a ton of detritus at the bottom of the beach. Caught that one as it washed up, along with a little stash of some clear."

He stands over a countertop, prepping his supplies and sanitizing the materials as Paisley seats herself in the spot where Adam had just motioned. Once I spot the collection of needles and the tattoo gun I start to feel a little bit woozy and take a seat on a wicker chair in the corner of the room. The reaction seems childish —I'm not afraid of needles—but the concept of having one digging into Paisley's arm repeatedly makes me a little bit nauseous.

"Keep that in your opposite hand, actually. It might help distract you if you're nervous, though honestly, your boyfriend looks closer to passing out than you do," Adam chuckles. "No judgment here, man. People pass out in this room more often than you'd think."

A few moments later, the tattoo gun begins to buzz, and we're marking something off Paisley's bucket list.

THIRTEEN

~ PAISLEY ~

If I wasn't already dying, my mother would kill me for getting a tattoo.

Fortunately, I am—and she won't—which is perfect because seventeen minutes after I walk into Adam's shop I leave with a white bandage on my wrist and a bucket list that is one item lighter. Sweat pours down my neck from under my wig, the drilling of the tattoo needle causing me more acute anxiety than my first chemotherapy treatment. On top of that, I might have broken Mitchell's fingers with my ferocious stress-ball squeezing. I can tell by the way he wrings the skin; red and purple fingerprints in the sandy hue of his complexion. There's a little bit of guilt that flows through me, but something about having him there made the pain more bearable. As if in some way we were able to share it so it didn't hurt as much as it could have.

Maybe he could do that for the cancer too.

I shrug the thought off as a selfish endeavor.

Georgia squeals when Mitchell and I return to the car, demanding that I peel away the tape and let her see the design. I shove my tingling arm over the top of Taryn's lap to the other side of the Escape, my head throbbing in time with my arm from adrenaline and grinding my teeth. She must rip off half my skin in the process of unfastening the adhesive, Mitchell turning over the engine and pulling from the gravel parking space in time with her tugs on the transparent tape. I close my eyes as the air conditioning pours over me in a blast and Georgia rubs her finger softly over the inky blotch underneath.

"I love it, Ley. I didn't think that place did real tattoos." Taryn pats the gauze back into place and re-sticks the tape. "I might have gotten one too if there would've been time."

I rest my pulsating arm across my stomach as we cruise down the road toward Cavendish Mini Putt, goosebumps prickling my skin from the cold air.

"Fair enough."

Black lampposts and baskets of hanging pink and purple annuals line the roadway, whizzing by as Mitchell takes us down Parkway. Fields of Holsteins dot the road as we venture to the edge of the tourist area, offering a scenic country boundary to Partridge Island's quiet geographical remains. While I watch this world blow past, Dean fiddles with the radio, tuning the station between oldies hits and alternative rock, flipping back and forth on the channels as if he's trying to hear both bits at once. My heart feels slow, a drum about to die out at the end of a song, and I find it hard to catch my breath for a minute.

Mitchell curses as he slows to pull into the empty parking lot of the mini golf place. The building is clearly locked up, lights off, the gate around the course closed with a big sign hanging from the post.

CLOSED FOR REPAIRS

There's a collective silence, and inside of it, they're all waiting for me to say something. This was on my list, after all, but thanks to my sudden exhaustion, I'm not heartbroken by the bump in our plans.

"Guess we'll have to start the Canada Day party early? When we get back on the cottage wireless we can always look up somewhere else to play tomorrow or something." I shrug. "Not really any other option today. Plus a drink sounds pretty good right about now."

Nobody disagrees, and so back we go, eastward.

The drive is pretty along the shore, all white-capped waves and red beaches yawning along the coastline while winding roads and wiggling side paths lead in all different directions. We cruise past at least twenty fields of potatoes and corn, a couple of pastures of horses, and an interesting heritage building with a rooftop patio where a fiddler and band are playing some kind of Celtic reel. The music floats through the airwaves and into the open windows of the Escape, accenting the sounds of the radio that Dean will not stop toying with.

Forty minutes later, I'm sitting on the patio with Mitchell and he's putting an ice cold beer in my outstretched hand. "Cheers."

I clink the bottom of the dark glass against the side of his as he takes a seat facing out over the grassy hill. We swig silently, watching distant boats bob along the Gulf, and after a few minutes draw past, I finally realize we've been left to our own devices for the time being.

"Where is everyone?" I lick the ribbed rim of the bottle.

"Taryn's upstairs texting some girl and Dean and Georgia are making dinner. They're kind of cute, in a too-much-sugar kind of way."

"Taryn's been texting that girl an awful lot since last night," I muse, gulping down another mouthful of yeasty liquid. The alcohol trickles through my system, numbing the residual pain in my arm and on my sunburned skin.

"Taryn has something she isn't telling us." Mitchell sloshes the beer around in his bottle, his eyes never quite meeting my own. He seems embarrassed to be out here alone with me as if he's discreetly asked everyone else for this privacy but he doesn't want me to know.

"What do you mean?"

"She's a lesbian, Paisley. Haven't you noticed her fascination with Summer Parkinson the last couple of months?"

"Summer has rainbow hair. It's hard not to be fascinated with that."

Mitchell snorts, his bottle already almost empty. He knows I'm aware of what he means, and clearly, he doesn't feel the need to discuss the matter any further.

"I wonder why she isn't telling us," I ponder aloud, shuffling my position in the plastic chair. "I always thought we told each other everything. She knows we would support her."

"I don't think that's the issue. Maybe she just isn't ready to admit it to herself." There's a cold bit of irony in the statement as if Mitchell can read my mind and my feelings alike. I'm not ready to admit my desire for an even closer relationship with him, and maybe I still wouldn't be if cancer wasn't a part of the situation. I've never been particularly interested in having a boyfriend, the majority of my high school career spent juggling hospital visits, homework, and an inordinate amount of sick days. I guess I never really had time—and now that saying is working against me in a whole other way.

Mitchell sucks back the last of his beer in silence as I nurse mine carefully, the chill from the fridge quickly dwindling to leave the dregs in a warm sort of unpleasantness. We only have so much to drink, so I don't waste it, hauling the beverage back as I pick the tape covering my tattoo.

"You know, I meant everything I said at graduation. And the other night, you know, before we got interrupted." Mitchell nearly whispers the words, the chirping of crickets accompanying his statement. My heart responds before my head, an arrhythmic beating pressing on my intoxicated blood vessels. It makes me a little bit dizzy.

"You did?"

"I still do, Paisley. I want to do this. I want to be with you." His eyes finally capture my own, and we look at each other as if he hasn't caused an earthquake inside both of our bodies.

"I know you think—"

Mitchell cuts me off.

"Don't even try to say that you know I want this because every little piece of me is screaming for you to agree. I can tell you—hell, the way you look at me when you think I can't tell, the way you brush up against me just to get the feel of it. You can't keep denying the things you want and I hate begging to send you reminders."

He places the empty beer bottle on the patio wood with a muted clunk as I woefully admit to myself that he isn't even close to being wrong. As I do so, a hawk lazily circles above the clump of trees to our right, eavesdropping on our moment as a reminder we aren't really alone.

"When I think about hurting you, it makes me physically ill. It feels like I'm dying over and over again," I admit. The words come out before my internal filter considers censoring, and Mitchell runs a hand through his hair before responding. My heart has migrated to my throat, even though he's made it abundantly clear I have no reason to be worried.

"You're hurting me by trying to ignore this."

"I'm not trying to ignore anything on purpose. I just—" I cut myself off and search for the right words, all of my vocabulary billowing inside my brain like helium-filled balloons. "I'm dying. I could die tomorrow. I don't want to break your heart. I've seen you with a broken heart before, and I can't allow myself to be the cause of it. That alone would probably kill me."

There is a pregnant pause.

"Do you love me?"

The screen door flies open, Georgia holding a giant serving bowl filled to the rim with tortellini and red sauce.

"Dean's got the plates and forks, Taryn's bringing out the two bottles of wine she stole from Joffre's stash. As the responsible one of the group, I demand we all eat at least some of something before the excessive drinking begins."

She places the yellow and blue striped terrine on the glass of the outdoor table, the smell of Parmesan and marinara floating on the airwaves. My stomach growls a violent response as Dean and Taryn crash their way out of the cottage. Mitchell, a little bit frustrated at the untimely interruption, glances at me and leans over the arm of his chair as he sidles it up to the food.

"Take your time with the answer. I'm not going anywhere."

He isn't, but I am.

FOURTEEN

~ PAISLEY ~

A couple of hours later, we've exhausted dinner, two bottles of wine, and the rest of a case of beer.

Glasses of all shapes and sizes rest on the top of the table and attend our hands as we draw into the night with intoxicated expectation and stomachs full of cheese-stuffed pasta. The conversation remains light: searching for miniature golf places that aren't shut down, remembering the good old days of high school, ignoring any talk about the future for presumed fear that I might be reminded that I'm not going to have one.

It's not like I don't know that already, and ignoring it doesn't change reality.

To complement the fading rose color of the setting sun, Dean drags out a bottle of some hard liquor, a couple of joints, and a military grade flashlight from the drawer of the kitchen island. Stars have already begun to speckle the sky like a knitted indigo blanket, the little patches of light serving as the holes between the cast stitches, telling the five of us that the time for setting up a bonfire is now. As we gather the dishes to pile into the kitchen, Georgia carefully loads the dishwasher, and Mitchell brushes my bare arm with his open palm. He's testing my resistance, and with all the beer sloshing around, I'm sure he quickly realizes there isn't anything stopping me.

I've never been drunk before, but I only assume the sensation I'm feeling is a prime example of the way too much alcohol in a short period can make someone feel. My head is fuzzy, my thought processes a little bit delayed, the pain from my burn and the flower tattoo having long since dissolved into an overwhelming sensation of nothingness. When I walk, I swear I'm floating, my feet hovering over the wooden veranda boards, and strands of unmowed lawn tickle my bare toes in flip-flops. My emotions are dictating too many things, like that I want to admit to Mitchell that I probably do love him.

I need a little bit more to drink to get those words out.

We follow Dean and the darkness in a single file line, down over the gully and through long seagrass to populate a red sand beach at the edge of the property. The flashlight makes a stark beam of light as he leads the way, the smoke from one of his cigarettes curling up into the eve and melting as part of the sky. Mitchell and I have faded somewhere into the background, his cell phone lighting our way. We're at least twenty paces behind Taryn, who is singing some old camp song from out childhood and reminding us that ever since that time we've all started falling apart, crumbling from kids to uncertain adults.

I trip over a root and stumble into Mitchell's arm, an unre-strained giggle leaping from my throat. His skin feels warm underneath my touch, a little zap of animal magnetism twirling between us as we stand in the dark and reason with ourselves. He doesn't let me go for longer than is probably necessary, but I don't mind the contact. It's different from the kind of sad touch that I'm used to in the form of bereaved hugs, stabbing needles, the silent feel of someone pitying your soul. Mitchell holds me because he wants to hold me and because both of our defenses are starting to wear down.

Then it hits me like a bolt of lightning. I want to try this, and I want to be with him. I don't care that we don't have a lot of time. We're both breaking our hearts by not letting our last moments together be the best ones we've experienced.

"Come on, slowpokes!" Dean calls from somewhere in the depths of the dusk. "There's already a fire pit built down here."

Mitchell's eyes reflect the stars.

"Mitchell?" I say his name like a question even though there isn't anything I'm about to ask. "I want to give this a chance. I mean, I don't think. I want to."

I'm so elegant in my speech when I've been drinking, a low fire beginning to crackle in the distance as I drag the syllables out. Little licks of orange, yellow, and red appear close to the sand and bounce off the water, and the smell of a freshly lit marijuana cigarette bumbles in the breeze. My wig prickles the skin on my cheeks, and I move to brush it away, but Mitchell gets there first.

"Are you serious?" His hand is on my neck now, and my heart starts to beat erratically in my chest, bumping against my ribs and my mastectomy bra. In between pulsations, I try not to think about what it would feel like to press my lips against Mitchell's own here under the Partridge Island sky.

However, within seconds, I don't have to wonder anymore.

It is Mitchell who moves first; he is like warm honey trickling over my mouth. His lips press my own in a gentle caress, waiting expectantly for my response, and the seconds seem to stop as I decipher the shock of the reality of what's happening. My brain yells at me, louder and louder until I finally hear the message: Mitchell is kissing me. Oh, my God.

Like instinct, my body responds as if it were both more alive than ever and created for the way Mitchell makes me feel. I shut my eyes and absorb the feeling of our intimacy, and as I relax, he pulls me into him closer, pushing his fingers against the back of my neck. A blanket of goosebumps covers me, and the reaction must send some subliminal signal to him because Mitchell deepens the kiss, letting his tongue slip against my own in a movement that could stop my heart if I allow it. Time slows as we melt together, two anonymous entities in the night, then it stops altogether when little fireworks start to erupt in my mind. There's an undertone of beer and drunken bravado in both of us; we own this moment, this night, and every constellation watching over the night sky in my head.

We pull away from the kiss at the same time, slowly, as if we're desperate for air but also each other. Mitchell's hands don't leave their place next to my throat, and though our lips have broken apart, he barely strays. Resting his forehead against my own, Mitchell stifles a little sigh in a cloudy silence where Dean, Taryn, and Georgia's voices punctuate the sound of rustling grass. Now that we have broken an intimate boundary we both are hesitant to go back to the space between us.

"We should probably get to the fire," Mitchell murmurs, the scent of sea salt twirling with smoke. I almost choke on my breath trying to respond.

"Maybe we can finish this later?" I offer in a bedroom voice that I never knew existed exiting my mouth. I wasn't aware of the six little words, when put together in the right order, could sound so suggestive.

"Mhmm. For now, let's just knock something else off that bucket list."

We tear ourselves apart, my nerves still humming, and my brain screaming at me for more.

My heart might explode.

Mitchell slips his hand into my own for the rest of the walk, turning our backs on the lights coming from the cottage kitchen window. Once my feet hit the sand, I can comprehend just how drunk I am. But this is my night, my last party, perhaps. The worst thing that can happen is I get alcohol poisoning and die. Screw the slow demise of cancer.

We separate our hands once we get into the illuminated glow of the fire, something still not quite ready for an official acknowledgment.

"You two! I thought we'd lost you." Georgia laughs, inhaling deeply on her marijuana cigarette. The bonfire is a warm, burning red with a tawny base, Dean prodding some of the wood with a long stick as smoke curls from the tips with his smile. As I take a wobbling seat next to Taryn, I replace Mitchell's fingers with a quart of something strong that tastes like burnt cinnamon and cough syrup.

"Just had a moment. Everything's okay. Paisley might be a little more out of it a bit faster than we anticipated."

Georgia purses her lips; she wants to tell Mitchell to stop lying.

The night is tranquil on the beach, private and unmoving except for the undulation of the waves hitting off the sandy shoreline. We drink and smoke in a modified silence, the secrets between us all growing with every interaction. Although Georgia and Dean have been outed with their relationship, Mitchell and I seem to be just on the verge of starting something. And Taryn, well, I don't think any of us have any idea what's going on with her anymore.

"Why don't we play Truth or Dare?" Georgia asks, letting the question hang out into the clothesline of the sky. "Keep things interesting."

"You really want us to willingly ask you a bunch of questions about what the hell is going on with you and Dean? You're offering up that power to us?" Taryn takes a swig from a wine bottle, the little bit of liquid left sloshing in the bottom.

"You don't think we have a bunch of questions of our own?" Georgia wrinkles her brow and tosses the butt of her joint into the fire. "Just for that statement, you get to go first, and I say you pick truth and I get to ask you the question."

"What if I want to pick dare?"

"Then I dare you to tell me the truth about who you've been texting the whole drive up here."

Here comes Georgia, playing hardball. We all know how she

can get when she's been drinking, and Dean takes it upon himself to stop her in her tracks.

"Don't you think that since this is Paisley's gathering that she should get to pick first? I mean, this whole thing was supposed to be for her benefit, you know?"

Georgia shuffles on her piece of driftwood, reaching out to Dean for the bottle of whatever he is drinking. I take a long drag of the spicy liquor before placing the glass container down in the sand, making a divot.

"Alright. I'll take that," I slur. "I mean, I'll go, but I want to start out with a hella important truth question for you all. What's the one thing you're going to remember about me? You can only pick one, so don't qualify your statement by giving me any of the 'oh, I don't know, there's too many things' bullshit. The best answer gets to ask me Truth or Dare."

Mitchell nearly coughs up a lungful of rum at my cursing, probably because the terminology sounds strange coming from my drunken mouth.

"God, Paisley, way to turn this into a morbid affair." Taryn leans forward into the fire, a cigarette in her hand, and the tip of it picks up the tiniest flame. "But I've got something that immediately comes to mind. Remember that time you tried out for the city choir?"

My immediate reaction is to turn around and slap Mitchell across the chest for giving away my secret.

"You ass! You said you never told anyone!"

Mitchell rubs his chest with a feigned hurt expression, chuckling.

"I didn't! I swear! There's an even better explanation for this one. Taryn, quick, before she hits me again."

But Taryn is drunk laughing too hard to get the words out, so Dean has to fill in.

"Paisley, Taryn was there too. Did you know that she can sing? Because apparently, that's something. I mean, not good enough to make city choir but good enough to make dogs howl. It's quite a skill."

We all break into a pile of laughter, sipping away at our drinks and sucking ono the various smokes we had smuggled onto the island. It was the perfect start to a perfect night, the five of us sitting for what might be the last time, together under the same sky and watching the same big moon roll across the canvas of the night.

It's nearly midnight by the time I start to relinquish my party persona to whichever god is in charge of watching over underage inebriation. I'm sitting on a piece of driftwood, Mitchell to one side and Taryn to the other, and a slow burning fire in front of me with appendages reaching to scorch the sky. We've almost polished off all of the clear liquid Dean snuck in from home, passing the bottle around the circle to share our intoxicated germs, the movement of the drink coinciding near the end with the shifting of the last of the marijuana. I like being high better than being drunk, but right now I'm both, and it feels pretty damn wonderful.

But the day has been long.

"Guys, I love you but think it's time—bedtime. I require a bed and now is the time. Goodbye, bitches." The words fall out of my mouth in bits as I stare at the silhouette of a girl I think is Georgia. "Have super fun times. But not too many super fun times without me. I'll be mad if you have them all and there are none left over."

At least those are the words in my head. I can't be certain they're the words I say out loud. Fortunately, Taryn understands that if I'm left to my own devices, I might not find the cottage up the hill; I need an escort. That escort is a drunk version of Mitchell and he half-carries me back up the hill while I laugh maniacally and watch little-multicolored hallucinations creep along in the dark.

In my next moment of clarity, I'm back at the cottage and Mitchell is holding the door open. My sandals are in my hands, and my head is throbbing a hammered symphony of tightened blood vessels. As I walk through the threshold and into the kitchen, my brain throws an idea at me: if cancer and the alcohol are having some sort of battle for my brain cells.

I drop my sandals on the tile with two little slaps, holding onto the kitchen island, so I don't fall. My legs are unsteady, and my knees are covered in wet grass and dry dirt.

The screen door slams.

Mitchell walks toward me, a little waiver in his step, and opens his mouth to say something. There's the sound of speech but my mind is all over the place, and the words don't register. The world is underwater, and I can't tell if I'm swimming to safety or drowning in the middle of the ocean. Then my brain starts to scream at me, a high pitched voice with a single tone that I decipher to mean Mitchell can stop me from sinking to the bottom of the rhetorical pool.

So I fall into him, a desperate fervor welling up in my veins. One shaky hand grabs the back of his neck, the other slides up underneath the hem of his shirt, and my fingers press him down toward me. Mitchell smells like warm beer, dewdrops, and the ocean; our lips connect like two flames, red-hot and primed for endurance. I make a small and subtle whining sound, the pleasure from his skin touching mine sinking through my mouth and down to paint the rest of my body.

"Paisley, we're drunk," he mumbles into my lips, around the same second I try to slip my tongue against his own.

"I know, and amazingly it makes everything feel better."

In one fell swoop, Mitchell lifts me up by the back of my thighs, plunks me down on the cool countertop, and buries his face in my neck.

"It does, but kissing you sober felt pretty damn good too." He nips at my earlobe, pushing away my wig to presumably give him better access. Liquor makes us bold, unrelenting and lacking boundaries—those divided lines we crossed when my mind decided I needed to make up for lost time.

"We've got this whole place, you know," I murmur, digging my fingers into the top seam of his shorts. My grasp is ragged, and I fumble with the button.

"What are you thinking?" Mitchell divides himself from me and stares restlessly into my eyes until he answers his own question. My face must have given me away, even though I can't feel it. "Wait, I know what you're thinking. I like this side of you. I like you. I like when you lose control a little bit."

I pop his button open and slip down the zipper, the fabric hanging from his hips.

"Paisley," he mumbles. I creep my fingers under the elastic of his boxer briefs, and Mitchell grabs my hands. "Paisley. Paisley, okay, hold up. You're drunk. I'm drunk. Let's not start out like this. I mean, I want to, but this seems wrong."

He's right. What the hell am I doing?

"Sorry, I just—" I start to stutter. "I'm just excited to do this, I guess. But every second counts, you know."

Mitchell extends his hand and helps me down from the counter before adjusting his clothing.

"Go get in your pajamas and close the door to your bedroom. Then come upstairs."

"Close the door?"

"If your door's closed everyone will assume you've passed out in your bed. Right now I'd really rather if you passed out in mine."

The sensation of my face flushing crawls over me, and I can't tell if it's because of his bluntness or because of all the alcohol.

"Are you just trying to get me in bed?"

"Obviously. Upstairs. Five minutes." Mitchell traipses to the staircase, halfway up before I move. Even then the action happens slowly, dragging my fingers along the walls for guidance until I find the bed. If I only rest for a minute, maybe the sick feeling will go away. Then again, if I get under the covers, I might pass out.

I force myself to dig through my bag to find a pair of cotton shorts and a plain pink tank top, both of which I shove onto my body unceremoniously. As I close my bedroom door and step back out into the kitchen light, the brightness blaring holes in my eyes, the staircase strikes me as a mountain—tall and high and overwhelming. Slowly, but surely, I crawl up over the ascending wood planks. Mitchell's room is at the top of the steps.

I don't even need to knock; clomping on the floor seems to be enough. The entryway opens, and I stare up at the muscular 'v' running past Mitchell's bare chest.

"You look cute, Ley. Get in bed before you pass out."

He puts out a hand, but I'm too wobbly to let go of the hardwood.

"What's with the demanding tone?" I flub out the words, tripping on my own tongue. "Don't tell me how to live."

"You're sitting on the floor and your shirt's on backward."

Normally I would feel embarrassed but being drunk off my ass has made me no longer give a crap.

"Just—I'll get there. I just need to stop moving for a second. Spinning. I'm spinning."

"You're not moving."

"Let's go swimming. I want to touch the ocean. It makes sense, Mitchell. The world is so small but also so big and watery."

I rest my head down on the hallway floor, the surface cool with central air. The thought comes to me to try and clarify my words but the whole cottage is wobbling around me, making lazy circles above my head. I consider that maybe closing my eyes will make it go away, but this only throws me into a state of partial consciousness. The walls dance as hands pick me up, resting my body on a familiar chest as it weaves through the bedroom. The sheets feel warm on my skin, and within seconds I fade away entirely.

FIFTEEN

~ PAISLEY ~

Taryn told me there's a store in one of the tourist malls that sells lobster flavored chips, and I dream about how I imagine they would taste.

As I sit on a picnic table in the middle of a grassy field, the taste of salt runs over my tongue, prickling my taste buds with a sensation remnant of the beach water. Waves of crystal blue water roll past me, licking at my feet from my perch on the top, a light breeze messing up my real hair, tangled around my shoulders in waves. It all seems perfectly normal for an island in the middle of the ocean; my dream-self occupied with shoving chip after chip in my mouth. The more I eat, the less I'm satisfied. Maybe this says something about the way I perceive life as a whole. If I had the energy to look up the meaning in a dream dictionary, I bet I would find a whole webpage about unfinished business and thus be able to relate it back to my bucket list.

The dream ends abruptly mid-crunch of a particularly large chip, an uncomfortable and pressurized rumble in my stomach waking me. The early morning light streams through the window onto Mitchell's bare back, warming his golden skin into the light hide color of a summer deer. It only takes another second for the sound of digestion to get caught in my throat, and it's almost too late before it hits me that I'm going to get sick. Thankfully there's a wastebasket next to Mitchell's bed and I grab it just in time, waking him from his sleep with the sound of me puking my guts out. I'm not as embarrassed this time as I was when we were at the boardwalk. It has something to do with the repetitive nature of the action, knowing that even after all that he still wants to try and be with me.

"Ley? Are you okay?" Mitchell's words are sleepy, but his tone is concerned. The blankets shift around me as he rolls over, presumably to look at what's going on. At first, I can't respond, spitting out disgusting sputum and trying to get my voice back. After a second I'm pretty sure that I'm going to be all right, then the churning restarts in my stomach, more and more liquid pouring out of my mouth, all acid and bile and leftover alcohol. It happens at least five times in a row, hard and heaving sicknesses that tear at my muscles and strains my body until I'm leaning over the side of the mattress vomiting nothing at all except the air from my insides.

Mitchell places a soft hand on my back. "I'm going to get help."

I want to tell him not to bother, that I don't want the others to see me like this with puke on my lips and no wig and no bra. Instead, Mitchell crawls out of bed past me, opens the door, and dashes down the staircase in his shorts from last night and no shirt. His feet slap against the laminate floor.

"G? Do we have like, a bucket or something?" His murmuring voice travels along with his footsteps, and I can picture the look on Georgia's face as she gets asked the question.

"Maybe, I'm sure somewhere in here. I mean, there's a mop in the closet." Georgia's voice floats up the staircase. "What's going on? Are you that hungover?"

"I'm fine, but Paisley's throwing up like a lot."

"Jesus Christ." It's Taryn, and she sounds worried. There are a few other grumbles and whispers and clangs as a closet door opens and shut in the kitchen. Seconds later quick footsteps ascend the staircase, and she appears in the doorway with a bucket and a glass of water. My eyes start to water as the embarrassment that goes along with this situation comes to me—I didn't want everyone to figure out I'd spent the night in Mitchell's bed. Worse yet, I don't want them to think something happened between us already. I don't know why it bothers me so much, because they'd all be more than happy for us at least trying to have some semblance of normalcy, but it's the kind of thing I need to keep private and hold on to until I go to my grave.

"Hey, Ley. Are you feeling all right? Dean's getting us some clean towels and I've got you an empty bucket." Taryn looks no worse for wear, and I'm jealous of her casually pink cheeks and the way she's able to fill out her tank top properly like a woman should according to modern media.

"Don't call Georgia's dad," I croak, placing the trashcan gently on the floor and rolling over on the sheets to prop myself up against the wall. "I don't want me drinking too much to ruin this whole thing for all the rest of you. I was stupid; I made a stupid decision."

"Stop worrying, Paisley. It happens to everyone sometimes."

"We're supposed to be on vacation; you're not supposed to be babysitting me. It's all right, really. I'm sure I'll be okay if I just sleep this off a little bit longer."

"We were just going to head into town, but maybe we should stay around here." Taryn shrugs and turns her head to look out the chalet windows, a bright blue morning waiting to be used to full advantage. She checked the weather obsessively last night, and Partridge Island is supposed to be hot for the rest of the week— thirty degrees Celsius and pushing. It would be unfortunate for everyone to miss a good day in town or at the beach because I'm an idiot and can't handle something as simple as consuming alcohol.

"You guys go. I'll stay here with her." Mitchell stands in the doorway with a handful of wet rags. "We have some things we probably need to talk about. Plus, it's already past noon. If you guys want to get there, you'll probably have to leave soon." He steps carefully along the floor as if the noise of the boards will break my bones, and hands me a moistened cloth to wipe my mouth. I tell from the mirror across the room that I'm pale and off-white, the color of a smoker's teeth, my sunken-in face making the bed around me look larger-than-life. My lips are blood red like a child with a mother's lipstick. Despite all of these signs of illness, I am feeling significantly better now that I've gotten rid of everything in my stomach.

"Mitchell made it sound like World War Three up here." Taryn smiles, handing me the glass of water. "Now he's just trying to get rid of us."

"He's always overreacting. I was trying to tell him I'm fine but he ran off before I could get the words out. Alarmist." I offer a weak smile, sigh, and take a sip from the tall cup. "Maybe the drinking part of the list wasn't the best idea."

"How are you feeling other than that?" Mitchell nods, taking a seat at the end of the bed.

"You mean other than the cancer part?" I take another small drink of water, then reach over to place the rest on the nightstand.

"Well, *that* if you want to talk about it. If not, the part about how you spent the night in bed with Mitchell." Taryn squeezes my leg. "Otherwise, I'll just tell you that Dean and Georgia haven't abandoned you in your hour of need, but are instead downstairs Googling every possible remedy for a hangover ever."

Mitchell punches Taryn in the shoulder, and she smiles; I can't help that I smile back, the coolness of the wet dishcloths from the kitchen feeling soothing against my warm skin.

"Nothing happened." The words crawl from my mouth, looking at Mitchell for confirmation about what I'm going to say. "We were both messed up. But I told him we would try this whole being together thing. We're just fast-forwarding a little bit. It's going to be all thunder and lightning and fury like in the movies."

Taryn replies with something, her lips moving, but the sound not making it through my ears enough to be processed by my brain.

There's a ringing tone that echoes in my head, gradually getting louder and louder, before that loose, watery feeling rises again in my stomach. It feels as if lava is brewing in my insides, even though I don't think there's anything left in there to come out, and she stops mid-sentence while I start dry heaving, gasping for air with pained lungs.

Georgia's shadow peeks in the door and catches the corner of my eye, but I spot the Taryn, and Mitchell shoo her away after handing her the wastebasket half full of my throw up.

A minute later, I wipe errant tears from my eyes, the salty wetness rolling down my cheeks from the effort of convulsing.

"Please, just go with Dean and Georgia. I swear I'll be fine. Having a bunch of people stick around to watch me throw up isn't exactly going to make me any more comfortable. Plus, Mitchell's already taken my vomiting virginity the other day when I went to get the tattoo."

"Wait, you were this sick then too? Paisley, you've got to tell us these things. Georgia's dad needs to know if you're getting ill every day." Taryn glares at Mitchell who only shrugs as I brush my hand against the corner of my mouth.

"That's precisely why I didn't want you all to know. This is normal, Tee. This is what my life is like. I don't want to alarm anyone. I want you all to have fun and enjoy the rest of the time we have left together. And if that means doing a few things without me, that's okay too. Mitchell and I have some things to talk about that we don't need an audience for."

Taryn rises from the bed, turning to look at Mitchell standing in the doorway.

"If you're sure."

Mitchell nods. "I'm sure."

I breathe a sigh of relief before sinking into the pillows.

SIXTEEN

~ MITCHELL ~

The Cancer Canada website says that light alcohol consumption should not harm a patient under medical treatment.

It neglects to tell me if it will harm an eighteen-year-old girl with late-stage brain cancer who is also post-mastectomy. If only there were a help section on the site, somewhere, I could type in my question to ease my anxious mind, but everywhere suggests contacting a medical professional with questions. The only medical professional we have is Georgia's dad, and Paisley wants nothing to do with him. She's still convinced she's both fine, and invincible. Or at least that's what she lets us think.

Paisley confirmed, with Georgia, that she didn't want to keep the rest of us cooped up in the cottage on such a beautiful day, and of course, I wasn't planning on leaving her alone in the cottage in her state. I'd rather spend some sober time alone with Paisley rather than browse a market for yet another Partridge Island embroidered sweater. So, with much reluctance and the reiteration of her father's cell phone number, Georgia, Taryn, and Dean take my keys and head off for the town while I make my way back up to bed with my laptop in tow.

We rest both on top of and underneath the disheveled covers, little-pointed flowers on the bed sheets like a flat garden. Paisley lightly snores with her wig crumpled up and lopsided, while I read medical articles on the Cancer And You website that is enough to turn my stomach. Every once and awhile I'll lean over to check and make sure she's still breathing—as if she's a pet that we're waiting to pass quietly in their sleep.

Paisley doesn't know that I was still standing outside the door while she spoke to Georgia, keeping my back pressed up against the muted, blue paint of the hallway. Of course, Georgia's eagle eyes caught me and waved me away, but I couldn't bring myself to wander too far once Paisley started getting sick again. The sound pricked at my heart; needles into proud flesh.

The day fades slowly from a crisp periwinkle to a tessellation of pinks, purples, and oranges. Every time my eyes gaze upward, the sky is a different color, the hues all the same and different at the same time. It's almost eight when I get a text from Dean saying he's just leaving town from taking the girls to dinner, and I can't believe how much time has passed since I started staring at the computer screen. The little jingle of my phone must reach Paisley in a place of light sleep because as I'm typing back a response, her toes wiggle under the sheets.

"Mitchell?" Her voice is small as she rolls over, black hair splayed in the light of my dull bedside lamp.

"I'm right here." I press send, and the message zooms away. "How are you feeling? Georgia left a glass of water and an orange on the nightstand. They'll be home in an hour or so."

Paisley pulls herself into a sitting position, a little bit of rose-coloring in her cheeks. She tries to adjust her wig that's now been rustled around, the article badly in need of a brush and probably a rest from wear. Her hand slips up and underneath it, rubbing the hidden scalp back and forth. I've never considered that wearing it is probably itchy after a while.

"Just take it off, Ley."

She turns an even brighter shade of red.

"It's all right. Just need a little air under there."

I pause, a thought rolling like a heavy stone through my mind.

"Are you embarrassed?" I ask.

The question sits in the room, hanging on the wall like a photograph. She draws her hand from her head and looks away from me, watching a crow fly past the window.

"A little."

I adjust my seat to look at her, blankets wrapping around my legs like widened vines.

"Please don't be," I coax. "I've known you my whole life. You haven't scared me away yet. It's just hair."

I mean it, but I don't know how to make her believe it. She makes me feel like nobody else has—not the prep girls, not Melissa Ortiz or Isla Farmer during Seven Minutes in Heaven, not the women I've seen in movies who are supposed to make teenage boys wild. Paisley is a real girl, here before me, asking without words that I confirm for her that she still has value.

"I don't know. I'm not sure. It's probably best you—" Paisley shuffles the wig just far enough with her scratching that it falls off in a little black heap. "Oh."

Paisley stares at the clump in her lap and sighs, seemingly giving up.

Her hair is short, maybe an inch at the most, in varying degrees of thickness according to no particular pattern. The brassy, chestnut color of days gone past has faded into a chemical-induced mousy brown, even though the red still tries to peek through. A long scar, a reminder of her past surgeries to try and remove the tumor, streaks across the side of her head and up her hairline.

"Well, this is it then."

Paisley won't look at me, but I can tell her eyes are laced with tears. The pixie look actually kind of suits her face; shaped like a heart with big doe eyes. I might prefer the natural version of her to the wig, though it makes her more comfortable to have it on.

"Hey." I snap the laptop cover shut. "Don't cry. It's just me here."

Placing the device on the bed, I lean over and tip Paisley's chin toward me, the calloused ends of my fingers brushing against the soft skin of her face. The sensation makes my heart jump around in my chest, rattling between my ribs, just like it did the first time we kissed. Technically, that's still the only time, but not if I have anything to do with it. As I think I'd like to kiss her now, an errant drop falls on Paisley's cheek, her distant gaze staring holes through me.

"I feel so ugly. Like, I can't even describe it." Paisley's dark eyelashes hold speckles of leftover water. "You're a guy; you have short hair. I'm a girl. I'm supposed to have *something*. Something more than this peach fuzz. It won't even grow. Even though my chemo is over it still falls out all over the place."

Her voice crackles as she tries her best to hold back the rest of her tears.

"You're gorgeous." It feels like such a pithy offer, but I don't know what else to say. Much to my relief, Paisley stifles a giggle with a half-hearted sniff as I run my hands down her forearms to her tiny, bandaged wrist. I pick at the tape, pulling gently at the adhesive. She's watching me.

"You're just saying that."

"I'm not just saying that."

The bright blue of the tattooed flowers peeks out from underneath the sterile cloth. We both look at it, watching the slow exposure until the entire piece of art is revealed. My thumb brushes it carefully, the same way Paisley grazed Adam's arm when she first realized she could get a real tattoo.

"Did you really sit here all day with me?" She asks the question as if she doesn't already know the answer. I'd find it hard to believe that after the way she kissed me last night that she'd still have no idea what she does to me.

"I did."

"Even after everything stupid I did and said last night?"

"You were drunk. So was I. That's a thing that happens."

She offers me a tiny smile and reaches for her glass of water, probably now long since warm.

"It doesn't mean I didn't want to, Mitchell." Paisley looks at me mischievously and drinks. "I'm just; I don't know. I'm scared. I'm scared of everything. I woke up this morning and finally realized I'm going to die. Like, everything's going to go away all at once. I'm not going to be able to give up little pieces I'm comfortable with until I am left with nothing. It's just everything; nothing. One big bang."

She rubs her fingers over the flowers on her skin.

"I can't even pretend like I understand what that feels like, knowing you're going to die." I place the laptop on the floor and push myself up against the headboard next to her.

"Let me tell you a little secret—if you ever have the choice between knowing and not knowing—don't. Knowing is a special kind of hell."

Paisley places the glass back on the nightstand, empty. She hasn't just drained the glass; she's drained my heart. But instead of being empty it's filled entirely with something else: love, or something like it.

"Knowing means we have time," I offer with a shrug, looking over at her gathered up on the other side of the bed, the scent of jasmine wafting over the room." What is time, anyway? It's almost like we have an unlimited amount of it when I'm with you."

Paisley's lips are wet from drinking, the ruby red of them making me want to kiss them again. She turns her head, catching me staring, and grins.

"Mitchell, you're much more romantic than I anticipated you'd be."

Then there's that moment. You know it when you feel it. The instant that the stars align and you're on this extraordinary wavelength with the person right across from you. You're almost able to share your thoughts without speaking, actions without moving, and dreams without dreaming. There's a millisecond where electricity zaps like Canada Day fireworks and someone like me decides they have to take a chance.

I roll over on top of her, my hands pinned on the sides of her head as she shrinks down beneath me, burying herself in the enormity of my body against her own. The dark has started to befall the bedroom, a light midnight black that crawls over the field and in through the windows. The lamplight leaves contours on Paisley's face, little auburn highlights showing up in her hair. The words come naturally, formed in my heart rather than in my head, as I gaze down upon the small girl collected under my core.

Paisley tosses her wig on an accent chair, haphazardly aiming for the seat.

"Somewhere inside of me I've always loved you." My voice is low, with a gravelly tone that I don't quite expect.

"Are you just saying that to get me into bed?"

I laugh, and it feels like we have more than forty-five minutes until the others get home. It feels like we have a lifetime, infinity, and all in the galaxy that lies beyond.

"Ley, you've been in my bed for almost an entire day."

She playfully slaps at me.

"You know what I mean. I'm not complaining. I told you I want this. I'm just—honestly, I'm petrified."

"About what?" I knit my brow, sitting up to rest on my knees. The last bit of sunlight splashes her face in the pattern of stained glass.

"That you're going to see the rest of me and you're going to be disgusted."

"Oh God, really? Ley, I'm not going to be. I swear to God."

Paisley wriggles herself out from underneath me until she's standing barefoot on the bedroom floor.

"You see this outside, but it's not real, Mitchell."

My gaze falls over her, quizzically.

"Show me, then. Show me what's not real about you."

"Are you sure?" Paisley enquires, a little bit of hesitation in her voice.

"Always," I nod.

Paisley's shoulders heave at my response, the bones moving gently up and down as she forces an exhale. She flips her fingers under the bottom hem of her shirt, toying with the material, until her slender fingers pull up the fabric, exposing a plain black bra. The clothing comes to rest on the floor in a pile next to the discarded wig, and I adjust myself to face her, sitting on the side of the bed.

"These aren't real, Mitchell. This is fake. Filler. Something to make me feel like everyone else when I have a bathing suit on." Paisley gestures to her chest as she wraps her arms around her ribs, unclasping the band. "There's nothing here anymore. I'm blank."

The bra drops to the floor, exposing two long, matching scars where her breasts used to be.

My eyes graze over her lithe form carefully, as she stands there vulnerable to me, her thin waist calling for my hands to touch it. I move as if transfixed, looking at her face, standing up and crossing the room to close the gap she thinks she might have made between us. She looks braver and more wonderful in this moment than I ever could have expected.

"Just because a part of you is missing doesn't mean you're damaged. You're a fighter, Paisley. You let the world know you weren't going to give up that easily. You told cancer to go screw itself once. Maybe you'll do it again—who knows? All I know is right now you've done nothing—hear that, nothing—to make me want you any less than I wanted you before."

It takes Paisley about half a minute to absorb the undertones of the message I'm sending. I read the translation process on her face; the curl in her lips and the flush in her cheeks giving away the place where her mind is running to. But once she does, she takes it all in at once, a drowning breath of air before being completely submerged. Paisley throws all her weight at me, tackling me backward into the sheets. Her hands slide up the front of my shirt, viciously and tearing, as if we're going to lose each other at any second. Once she gets my shirt off, she sheds the remainder of her clothing, burying her face in the crevice of my neck.

Before I even think again about the magnitude of what's going to happen, we've already started.

SEVENTEEN

~ PAISLEY ~

Mitchell stands in front of the floor-length window entirely nude, a cigarette dangling from his mouth like he's god damned Adonis.

I've only been asleep for maybe ten minutes at best, dozing in and out while listening for the telltale sound of the screen door opening downstairs. It hasn't come yet, and Mitchell's side of the bed is empty, a mixture of marijuana and tobacco gating sucked into the pores of the bedroom. The smell reminds me of a type of incense Taryn used to have back in junior high: campfire, birthday cake, and pine needles all rolled into one.

I watch him smoke in silence, slowly and methodically, staring out into the field of milky stars and everlasting trees. My legs throb with a heaviness that can only be from one particular activity, and the curvature of Mitchell's spine and the way his hips connect to his thick thighs gives me a newly familiar tingle below my belly button. I can't help but think of how much has changed since we were kids —and how much has been altered just since we left home.

Sighing in satisfaction, I drag my bare legs through the sheets, untangling the limbs and enjoying the soft sensation. A hazy grey loop glides out of Mitchell's mouth and floats into the night as he turns to look at me, poised against the midnight blue canvas of the sky and edged in a silhouette that's created by the bedside lamp.

"How are you feeling?" The island breeze ruffles through Mitchell's hair as he stands in front of the partition, carefully fondling the lit stick with two fingers. I tumble the question over like beach stones in my mind. It feels like a loaded inquiry, even though I shouldn't assume as such.

"I—I don't know," I stammer, juggling the words in my mouth like they're made of cotton, a formal tone coming from my throat. "Fine? Is that a normal answer?"

He's trying not to laugh.

"I'm sorry, that was probably a stupid question. I'm not really sure what I expected you to say." Mitchell takes a last drag of the cigarette stub and blows the remnants out the screen, dabbing the filter in the ashtray on the nightstand. "It feels a little strange though, doesn't it? Like we've done something infinite?"

He turns to face me, and I'm staring—at all of him there, bare and before me.

"Here you go getting all romantic on me again." I don't bother clarifying that I like it, because it's obvious he already knows.

Mitchell sits on the edge of the sheets, the taut and lean muscles of his back rippling with the movement. "Can I get you anything? Smoke? Towel? Water? A beer?"

I throw a pillow at him for the last comment, and he laughs— one of my favorite sounds—kissing me on the forehead to punctuate his joke.

"You're shaking, Ley. Are you sure you're okay?"

Mitchell takes one of my hands in his, and when I peer down, the blue of my tattoo looks intensely bright against my pale skin. He's right; my hands are vibrating.

"I'm just overwhelmed. In a good way," I clarify, squeezing his flesh the best my weak fingers can muster. "I didn't really know what to expect. I've never really done anything, you know, with anyone. I've been sick most of high school while everyone else was out screwing around."

"Nerves and adrenaline, probably." Mitchell crawls underneath the sheets, half his body disappearing from view. "Honestly, I wouldn't have known you'd never been with anyone."

"Have you?"

I never thought to ask before now, and I'm not sure I want to know the answer. I like the intimate nature of Mitchell and I being each other's first—for me, he's also likely to be my last.

"No. I mean, there were a few Seven Minutes in Heaven in my past—" he puffs out his chest a little bit as if for some reason he should be proud of the accomplishment.

"I was at those parties, Mitchell," I remind him. "They don't count."

"But what if—"

"No!" I cut him off, laughing as he reaches over toward my bare thigh. "Arranged make-out festivals don't count. You have to have done it of your own accord."

"Then I guess this is a first for me too."

I smile to myself as an owl hoots from somewhere beyond the beach, the echo of which travels through the open window.

"Can we do it again?" I ask, the syllables of my request almost lost in the meekness of my voice. There's something silly about asking him this way, but I don't know how else to show my appreciation for what we've just experienced other than trying it a second time.

"We should probably wait until you at least stop shaking. And the others will be back soon. But I have plans for you later after everyone's gone to sleep."

The way he says it gives me goosebumps on my arms. I don't know if I'll be able to wait that long. I already feel neediness snaking through my body like I need to touch him and never let him go.

We lie there in the serenity of the moment before Mitchell asks me a question I would never have expected.

"Will you marry me?"

My first reaction is to laugh because I think he's joking. But as I glance over at him in the deepest part of the dark, Mitchell is entirely serious.

"What?" I stammer, rolling over to look at him face-on. "You're joking. Oh, my God. You're not joking, are you?"

"You wrote in that journal of yours that you're going to miss getting married." Mitchell reminds me. "I don't want you to miss anything. I'm in love with you, Ley. You're in love with me. Let's call up someone and get married here before real life makes us change our minds. I don't have a ring but I can get one. Or maybe instead I'll go back to Adam and get a tattoo to match yours. I kind of like that idea."

"You do remember that I'm going to die, right? Like, sooner rather than later?"

"I don't care."

I push myself up against the headboard of the bed; the flowered quilt tucked around my chest.

"But you'll never be married for the first time again. You're going to miss the party, the gifts, your mom crying over your first dance."

"I'm not going to miss them, Paisley. They're just things, traditions for other people that don't mean anything to me. The only thing I'm going to miss is you."

A thousand tiny thoughts run through my head, along with all the reasons I should say no. Logic dictates that I not let myself ruin Mitchell's life, not make plans too far into the future that serve as promises we won't be able to keep. But the softer part of myself, the one that came to Partridge Island with a bucket list and a journal of hopes and dreams, looks into the eyes of the boy from across the road and gives the most honest answer I could ever hope to provide.

"Yes."

"Yes, what?"

"Yes, I'll marry you, Mitchell Anders."

Mitchell immediately crashes across the bed, slamming his weight and his lips into me. We kiss for a long time, until my lips are chapped and raw with his fervor and passion, my fingers brushing along his nakedness and feeling the skin of the man to now be my husband. There's something there that wasn't there before, an intimacy that drives us to the second round of sex, but slower and more careful this time as if we're trying to savor every moment we can create together and put them all in the little shadow boxes of our minds.

Night surrounds us, and we surround each other.

Twenty minutes later, we're wrapped up in the quilt, a bedside lamp shining on our sheen and pleasure.

"Are you sure everything is fine? You're awfully pale. Are you feeling all right?" Mitchell eyes me carefully.

"I'm okay, really. I'm going to jump in the shower before everyone gets back." I curl myself out of the blankets I've been in all day, stretching a little and wincing at the tightness in my thighs.

"Sore?"

"A bit. In a good way. It's kind of hard to explain." Easing my way out of the bed, I discover my legs feel a little bit like jelly, and my brain is on the precipice of a migraine. Little speckles dot my peripheral vision. "Nothing a couple of Georgia's Tylenol down in the kitchen won't fix."

I reach for my shorts, discarded on the floor next to my wig, and try to pull them up over the lower half of my body. As I lean to slip them over my feet, my head gets woozy, and the world starts to tilt on the wrong axis. For a second, it almost seems like I've gotten up too fast after lying down for so long—a little vertigo as my ears rebalance—but then the colors on the walls melt together as if water has been poured over them. Instinctually, my hand goes out in search of a solid surface to steady me, but there's nothing around to catch my weight. Just as an imaginary icepick smashes into my skull, I crash to the floor in a confused pile of seizing body parts.

Pain radiates through my head and into my eyeballs, throbbing at my elbow joint where I've smashed it off the bedside table. Mitchell speaks, something in some language I'm no longer literate in, but the hum in my ears is so loud that I can't tell what he is saying. It buzzes like a thousand bumblebees, cruising around my head and building honeycombs in my ears. Even with my naked head resting on the floor they're everywhere, crawling over the inside of my brain.

In my mind, I'm screaming, scratching off my scalp to tear out the nerves that the tumor is encompassing. My fingers are bloody and raw, and clumps of what's left of my embarrassing hair hide under my nails. I have to get it out. It's going to kill me.

Then suddenly it is dark.

A soft and infinite kind of eve captures me, the kind that one might see when there's no moon, stars, or light in the sky for miles around. It's a deep ebony glow, both matte and glossy at the same time, taking over my body so that I don't even know it's there. It feels like it oozes over my skin; a gel. I turn around and around and around, but in every direction, I turn there's more nothing than there was before. Except there's a light as I move one way. A little white light with an open door.

I take a step toward it. This must be a mistake because as soon as I do, I'm falling and sleeping all at the same time, passing a prairie of everlasting night.

EIGHTEEN

~ MITCHELL ~

As if right on time, car doors slam outside, echoing off the walls of the cottage.

The bang of the trunk of the Escape corresponds with the start of Paisley's shaking, the crinkle of shopping bags and the slow shuffle of flip-flops clapping on bare heels toward the screen door. I don't know what time it is, but I do know I like the hollow sounds the crickets make—at least when it isn't being prefaced by someone having a seizure. I try my best to remember what I'd heard in commercials to do when someone is convulsing, put them somewhere safe where they can't hurt themselves, don't put anything in their mouth. If only Georgia would hurry up and get in here because I expect she would know what to do better than me.

Then there is a gigantic crash as Paisley falls off the bed and smashes into the floor, and I curse loudly and repeatedly as I fling myself across the sheets and onto the laminate next to her.

"Mitchell? You okay?" The screen door slams from downstairs, and I rip open the bedroom door with a force that can be felt in the beams of the cottage.

"Georgia? Call your dad!"

"What the hell's going on up there? Are you okay?"

"It's Paisley; she's just collapsed." My words all start to run together. "I think she's having some kind of seizure."

Georgia springs into action, stampeding up the steps two by two. I swear it takes her a single stride to cross the entire home, and maybe three to make it up the long staircase. She starts giving orders before her feet even hit the landing of the second floor, some part of her father's medical training ingrained in her as well.

"Mitchell, call Dad. Taryn, I need a couple of wet tea towels and some extra pillows. Dean, help me shift her to her side."

I lose the rest of the directions after that, my fingers grabbing Georgia's phone from her hand and punching in her passcode— 5683. She always told me love could unlock anything. Now it's obvious the numbers of her code spell out the word. Taryn bursts into the bedroom behind me, her bags left in the doorway, as I pound on Doctor Hart's contact information and hit the speaker-phone button to wait for the ringing. There's so much noise I hardly hear the phone ringing, and so I hastily leave Paisley in Georgia's hands and run down the stairs to the quiet kitchen.

One ring.

Two rings.

Three rings.

He picks up. There's laughter from the background and the sounds of a brass band, something loud and boisterous comes from the lead trumpet and blows holes in my ears amidst glasses clinking. He must be at a work function; a fancy one, I would guess.

"Hi, Georgia Peach. What's going on?" There's a little lilt to his voice that tells me he's been drinking, something that doesn't sit well knowing we might have a medical incident on our hands.

"Doctor Hart? It's Mitchell."

"Mitchell? Hi, son. Is something wrong? Hang on, let me step outside," he yells into the phone. "There's a bit of an affair going on for the doctors tonight."

There's the sound of static crumpling before the music slowly fades into the background. While I wait amidst the sound of footsteps and mumbled niceties, I lean against the kitchen island and pick timidly at the skin of an orange from the fruit bowl to occupy my mind until the other end of the phone quiets.

Taryn bounds up the stairs with pillows shoved under her arms.

"What's going on at the cottage? Is everything okay?" Georgia's father sounds concerned, the music now muted into a respectable decibel. "I assume if you're calling me this is more than just somebody having a hangover."

"Yeah, um— a bit more than that. Well, Paisley wasn't feeling well this morning, so I stayed home—at the cottage, I mean—with her. Georgia, Taryn, and Dean just got back, and she's had some sort of seizure. I don't really know what's happened, she started shaking, and she fell off the bed."

"Okay, Mitchell—Georgia knows a little about identifying a seizure. We had a dog who used to get them—"

"Jake, I remember." Golden lab. Totally irrelevant.

"Right. She will place Paisley somewhere she can't hurt herself. Blankets and pillows can help in tight spaces. Turn her onto her side so she doesn't aspirate."

"Georgia's already done all that, sir," I note, the outside of the orange rolling up in fragrant curls under my short fingernails. "She's up there cleaning right now. She just told me to call you. I guess maybe she thought you'd have some more advice."

"She's quick, that one." Doctor Hart chuckles, clearing his throat. "Going to make a hell of a nurse."

"I think so too, sir."

"Listen, Mitchell, I can't drive out there right now. If Georgia thinks Paisley needs someone to look at her, take her to the hospital and mention my name. Doctor Brossard is in the emergency tonight, Georgia's met him before. Honestly, though, seizures aren't that uncommon in an end-of-life scenario for terminal brain cancer. When she's conscious, and clear-headed find out if she's ever had one before."

"Okay." I peel off the rest of the orange rind and drop it onto the counter. My hands feel lost without something to occupy them; to make me feel like I'm doing anything. "Then what?"

There's a sigh on the other end.

"If she's feeling sick enough not to go anywhere and she's starting to have seizures, I'd say you need to take her home. Georgia isn't going to want to hear that, but it might be the safest option. I'm a podiatrist, Mitchell. I can only do so much here."

Georgia appears then, over my shoulder. Her hair is tied up in a lopsided bun, strands loose around her face. A pile of Easter egg-colored tea towels is bunched up in her hands, and she drops them into the sink atop the mountain of dishcloths from earlier this morning, weaving her way around the shopping scattered on the tile. Brushing her forearm over her face, Georgia gestures to the phone. Her eyes look even more tired than they did before.

"Hi, Dad." Georgia places the phone to her ear, deactivating the public speaker mode. "She's fine. Mitchell was here. She's a little confused, but she's awake."

There's a long pause where Georgia paces around the kitchen, walking back and forth to the stairs and down the hallway to Paisley's empty bedroom. Every second lasts a thousand minutes, the ticking of the living room clock only emphasizing the molasses-like speed of the passage of time. I don't know what to do in moments like these. The phone is being handled, Paisley has a room full of people upstairs, and I'm left standing in the kitchen like a useless idiot. I know what I have to do—I have to call it. We need to go home. This is only going to get worse.

"Georgia?" Dean's voice crawls through the cottage, reverberating off the cathedral ceilings of the one and a half storey. "We should pack it in."

I cast my eyes upward at him, and he is half hanging over the railing. My mother would say it's one of those teenage boy actions that prematurely ages her, and for a hair of a second, I finally understand what she means.

"She's on the phone with her dad. They're trying to figure out what to do."

Dean descends the stairs, a grim look on his face that I've never seen before. There's an undertone of anxiety in his expression, a tired wringing of his fingers and touching of his eyes giving away all his concern. He knows something's changed since we left—something other than the seizure—and I can only use my good instincts and best friend intuition to guess what it might be.

"I really think it's for the best. We're playing with fire."

"Just see what Doctor Hart—"

"Mitchell, she's petrified even though she won't admit it. She says she can't see out of one eye. Taryn's up there helping her get dressed. She needs to get home and her mom needs to call those care workers Paisley keeps sending away. I'll talk to Georgia and call Paisley's mom and dad while you go pack. We're driving back tonight."

"Okay. I'll do Paisley's room then I'll get a start on the kitchen."

Dean heaves a relieved sigh, pulling ice packets out from the freezer with one hand and digging out a cooler from under the sink with the other.

"Thanks."

Dean turns to face me once more.

"Mitchell? You didn't cause this, you know. Whatever you did, it didn't set off some irreversible chain of events. We gave her what she wanted—what she needed. And then on top of that, you gave her more."

His eyebrow goes up in disbelief.

"Oh please, you can't hide it from me. It's written all over your face. But you have to trust me; you didn't do this to her. The cancer did this. We're just trying to outrun it, you know."

"I wish I could believe that." A freezer bag drops into the bottom of an empty cooler with an echoed thud as I turn my back. "It finally caught up with us."

Blame grows in my mind like a weed, minuscule seeds scattered by the winds of over-thinking.

Dean's right, nothing I did could have caused all of this fallout —it's a part of who Paisley was before we ever decided to be together—but I still can't help the doubt. After all, it could only be cruel fate that would tear her away so quickly after we started making plans; little drops of metaphorical rain falling on my washed out parade. I'm being cursed for loving a girl, and on top of that, I'm being judged by the fact that I've been selfish with her time over the course of this vacation.

Or maybe I'm putting too much thought into fate and love and all things in between.

Dropping a half-full plastic cooler into the trunk of the Escape, I wipe at the back of my neck in the stifling summer evening. The inside of the cottage has a great air circulation system, but outside Partridge Island still has to be almost as hot as it was when the sun was hanging high in the sky. It's hard to breathe in this kind of thick humidity, and working to pack up the car in as little time as possible has my lungs begging for a second just to absorb enough oxygen to keep from passing out.

I plunk myself on the edge of the open trunk, heave a sigh, and stare blindly at the stars. There are a few constellations up there I pick out from when I was a kid and Nolan and I would go camping, but the indigo streaks running through the black sky are more distracting. Skinny tendrils of ghostly white curve their way alongside, a minimized look at the Milky Way from farther away than my mind can comprehend.

"Here's my bag, and another container of stuff from the kitchen. Georgia says everything in there is cleared out." Taryn appears from the side of the Escape and drops her ragged backpack in the gravel. "Paisley's on the couch with Dean eating the rest of the oranges from the fruit bowl. I helped her a little down the steps, but she's doing okay."

The night is silent once Taryn's voice stops, only small sounds escaping into the dark from inside the walls of the cottage.

"I can't believe we need to head back already. I mean, it's the best plan but it kind of sucks, you know?"

Taryn takes a seat next to me, digging her bare toes in the pebbles. I'm not sure how she stands walking on the unpaved driveway with nothing on her feet.

"It's kind of a wake-up call, don't you think? We're all floating around this island trying to pretend that everything's going to be fine but everything's not fine. Everything's falling apart no matter how hard we try to stick it all back. We're taping together sandcastles and hoping the tide doesn't come in."

I consider her statement for a moment, enjoying the encompassing nature of it all. Little lightning bugs dart in front of my eyes, making their way to the far trees in wiggling patterns as my heart pounds in my ears. The pattern is like an arrhythmic tympani.

"Paisley's scared, Taryn. I don't know how to help her."

"We're all scared of something, Mitchell. Unfortunately, her fear is the closest thing to us right now." She takes a deep breath of warm air, hoisting herself from the trunk ledge. "We can only manage so many things at one time. The statement is trite, but it's also true. I just don't know how much more I can let myself worry about her. I mean, it's inevitable, right?"

There's an undertone, a hint at something, that might be between the lines of what Taryn is implying.

"Speaking of, is there something I should know about you and the Internet girl?"

A faint little smile appears, accented by the moon and the rolling-in clouds.

"I don't really think now's the time for that. We've got something bigger to worry about." Taryn picks up her backpack from the ground and tosses it into the far corner of the trunk, burying the canvas beneath a disheveled pile of emergency blankets and shadows. "You should get to packing up your room so we can get out of here as soon as possible. Georgia called Paisley's mom and dad and neither of them are thrilled with us driving back home in the dark."

A little drop of water hits me in the forehead, then another on my shoulder. At first, it's just that symbolism for raining on my parade again, then the night sky starts sprinkling. A big grey cumulus sits on top of the south hill, threatening to storm.

By the time everything is packed up, and all the necessary phone calls have been conducted, the blackness above us has opened into a waterfall. The rain pounds against every hard surface, coating it in thick lakes of liquid, ripples rolling down the pavement to hidden storm gutters. My mother's voice echoes in my head a thousand times telling me to drive carefully, make sure I have my lights on, and leave enough space between me and the other vehicles in case someone starts hydroplaning. I asked Nolan once when I was younger if that voice went away as we grew up; he said it didn't. I finally believe him.

The Escape splashes through a particularly large puddle at the end of the drive before we pull out to join the empty parkway from the residential road. I use one free hand to load up the GPS to direct us straight to the Watts' house, the blue backlight bright in the midnight air. Paisley sits—nestled like a baby bird—in the passenger's seat, her empty eyes watching the windshield wipers swipe the glass on high speed. Under the hazy street lamps, I am blessed with a few reflections of her hair, that black wig back on her head to hide everything beneath.

Ten minutes must go by; then twenty. The parkway fades off into a highway to the Gulf Bridge heading back home.

When I flick my eyesight back in the rearview, Georgia is asleep on Dean's shoulder, and Taryn has her head buried in a hoodie, the country music station on the Escape low and crooning against the sharp splats.

"Mitchell?"

I almost don't hear her, but Paisley reaches over to touch my thigh, and the sensation of her hand gets my attention.

"How are you feeling?" I take my eyes off the quiet highway for just a second, looking over.

"I'm all right. Tired. My head feels like it's been run over by a truck and my vision's still cloudy. Thankfully it's my right eye so I still see you just fine."

A shy heat walks up to my neck and settles in my cheeks as I place a hand over her small one, holding it to my leg.

"You scared me, Ley."

"I'm sorry."

Thup, thup, thup go the wipers as a little flash of electricity hits somewhere out in the water. There's probably thunder too, but the rain and the road noise drown it out. As the weather rages, a question sits and festers in my mind like an abscess, leaking little bits of worry all over my consciousness.

"Are you scared?"

She snorts, a combination of laughter and perhaps surprise. The sound is meant to serve as an answer, a rhetorical and nonverbal confirmation. Paisley thinks if she says it out loud, maybe the ground will only swallow her whole and suffocate her in the dark, still waters of the night.

"You can admit it, you know. Without all the alcohol in your system."

She drums her fingers on my leg in response, giving me that same damn sly smile that knows how to break my heart.

"Can you do me a favor?" she asks suddenly, pulling her hand back from my lap to brush a bit of hair from her face. "It's nothing hard, and you don't really have to do anything at all physically. It's just something I have to ask."

"Okay." I agree with the strange request, but I don't really have any idea what I'm getting myself into. She makes everything seem so easy.

"Don't worry about me, Mitchell. You guys are all trying to put on this brave face for me. Mom and Dad try and do it as well. When you do, it only makes me worry about what's really going on inside your heads. It makes me have to feel anxious about how you're all going to move on. And that's selfish. And obnoxious."

She's crying, just a little, but enough that I can tell.

"You know that's just what people do, right?" A vehicle approaches from the other side of the double line, streaks of water on the windscreen making it look fragmented.

"But it's kind of—I don't know how to explain it. I've got this stabbing pain behind my eye—"

"Do I need to stop?" I try not to sound panicked, but I'm sure my voice goes up half an octave.

"No, no. Just probably should have brought some of those hospital-strength pain meds with me. I never thought I'd have to admit I need them."

A truck whooshes past, road water splattering hard against the side of the Escape.

"These past few days, Mitchell, they've been—you guys are amazing. And with you and the other night, I just, I don't know. I almost feel ready to go. Like I've had a bit more of a life to leave behind. And for you to say you want to marry me, well, that's just something else entirely. I guess now it isn't going to happen. I guess this is when I start falling apart."

"You always had something for us to keep with us, you know that." I flick down my high beams as another vehicle approaches. "It's not like you're going to be forgotten by any of us. Who knows, maybe we will all go out and get a matching tattoo. Like a memorial on our skin."

Paisley laughs, the sound soft as bells.

"You're sweet, Mitchell. Thank you. But maybe just you could do that. It would be more special that way. Something between the two of us."

The song on the radio switches over to something acoustic, a man's deep voice starting a melody in a quiet minor key.

Everything was grey, on the day you left me —
The rain fell for weeks on end —
But I knew the day that the storm went away that I'd —
Live on without you, live on without you —

I reach to turn the radio down, but she stops me, her warm fingers wrapping around my own larger ones. For a second, all the time in the world stands still, and we are in another moment where we are the only people that could exist. The squid-ink sky and the buttoned-up stars watch over our own country song as she smiles at me half-asleep—the last thing my eyes process before the oncoming vehicle smashes head-first into the Escape.

NINETEEN

~ PAISLEY ~

Jolting me out of my hazy leftover sleep is the feeling of my head crashing into the dashboard, the seatbelt locking against my shoulder and crunching against my collarbone. Two bright lights—headlights of the oncoming car—blind me, so close that my skin feels the heat coming off them, and early enough that I am haunted by the face of the other driver frantically trying to avoid us. He looks petrified, his life flashing before his eyes as our windshield wipers give another collection of futile slaps. It's as if the universe slows things down to make sure we see each other so that if there are any survivors, we can remain haunted by the way we stared into each other's ghosts.

There's time for that understanding later after everything ends.

I don't know what gets ripped away first, my body or my soul, but I certainly don't stop screaming from the moment of impact until the very second I lose consciousness. The latter feels like it doesn't happen fast enough, given the amount of pain that washes over my body. It's like getting a thousand rounds of chemotherapy all at the same time, that same thousand rounds complete with a thousand needles stabbing into my skin all over and tearing my flesh away from the bone. Of course, I don't fully understand that I'm the one making all the noise until just a second before I stop; the rest of the time my shouts are just background noise to the sounds of metal pulling away from other sheets of metal, muted by an orchestra of crashing. Everything moves in slow motion.

There's an unmistakable crunch of bones and joints and steel as the night is reduced into a burning pile of disaster. Loose objects from the change tray in the Escape turn from harmless trinkets into projectiles, a collection of coins, a mailbox key, and a Birch Valley bridge pass hitting me in the face and drawing blood from their velocity. Behind me, Georgia's and Dean's heads smash together, her arm flailing forward to protect her face, and some part of the car snaps the bone as if it were a twig. Everything else cascades together with a gloriously timed bolt of lightning and then drowns into a buzzing silence.

I can't see Taryn, but she's definitely behind me because her arms grabbed my seat and had yet to let go.

Amidst this all, the radio continues to play, somehow.

Little bird don't you want to sing me to sleep —
A black twilight reel and a soft summer sun —
Don't dry your eyes because we don't cry in the deep —
We just live on without you, live on without you —

A thick and heavy warmth trickles over me, a warm blanket to shelter me from the water dripping from the sky. Liquid runs along my mouth, a combination of rain and blood, the metallic taste of my own life getting caught up between my teeth. Around this time my eyes grow heavy, my chest hot and searing with steam and impact, and my hands lose their feeling, one after another, until my whole body tingles and then disappears.

Time passes, I assume, and I dream about flying. There's a general lightness of being that comes with the pictures in my mind, fluffy clouds all around me and a bright white light belonging to the sun warming my bare arms. I'm wearing an ivory lace dress, like the one I saw in a magazine once, a warm breeze tickling my legs and running through the little holes in the material. And I have hair, of all things, my thick brown locks running halfway down my back in heavy curls that blow around my face as I soar above Birch Valley like a bird. I'm able to see all of the houses of all of my friends, rooftops and Sawyer River all melting together in a familiar landscape reminiscent of my childhood.

When I wake up, I am on the pavement just outside of the Escape, looking over the accident scene rather than existing inside of it. It's an out-of-body experience, I tell myself, I'm in shock, and my brain is trying to protect me from the horrors of the circumstances by turning off some of my immediate panic. There's no other explanation for the calm that covers me, like taking a bubble bath in a deep tub after a long day. I suddenly realize I need to get up, need to help, need to make sure that no other vehicles smash into this wreckage, and so I pull myself to my feet, a little wobbly but the pain all gone. I can't help but wonder what level of shock I'm in that I'm up and walking around after just being involved in all of *that*. It doesn't matter right now. Nothing else matters except for saving my friends.

Rain pelts against the paint of the vehicles, the smoking blacktop, and hits the yellow line of the road as a bolt of lightning cracks across the midnight blue sky. The silence that follows afterward is deafening, the hot air searing against the water droplets and making them evaporate into a mist. In the misplaced tranquility, my ears listen for any tiny sound, but nothing comes to me save for the hiss of the wet engines all smashed up in the darkness. The night is still now, lights blaring like beacons off into the distance.

"Mitchell?" I croak out his name because my voice doesn't seem to want to allow me to yell any longer, my insides raw and broken after shouting at the top of my lungs. My skin searches for the feeling of his fingers in mine, but they aren't there anymore, instead a cool river of raindrops floats down my hand. Of course, I shouldn't have logically expected him to be so close to me—clearly, I was thrown from the car, the passenger door ajar with the roof caved all in on top of it, someone's unfamiliar body all crumpled and distorted in the space between.

"Mitchell?" I try again, the name leaving my lips this time but dissolving like sugar. The sensation is strange as if I've been muted.

I collect myself from the ground and rush toward the Escape. Peering into the cracked back window, I spot Dean trying frantically to free himself from his seatbelt, while Georgia is barely conscious with her head leaning on his shoulder. Her arm is broken, and she's wrapped between shifted luggage and a bloody blanket that I recognize as being one from her bed at home. Taryn is slumped against the door, head against the glass and bleeding. I reach for the handle to free her since she's the closest, but my fingers don't seem to be able to grasp the latch. I try again and again to close my hand around the plastic to pull it open, but it's almost as if there's nothing for me to hold. My fingers go right through the material, my limb a misty grey under the street lamps.

Wrinkling my brow, I slam my hand as hard as I can against the window, calling to Dean to open the door so I'm able to help Taryn. It's as if he can't hear me either, nor the sound of my hand crashing against the glass; there's nothing to indicate that I'm even present. I watch him open his own door latch and carefully extract Georgia from her seat on the middle of the bench, unwinding her from the detritus of the accident.

"Dean! Can't you hear me?"

The rain patters loudly on the metal, my only response.

"Georgia?"

There's no sound, nothing to indicate that I'm even present.

I run over to the opposite side of the car, note the missing driver's door, and crash my body into the gully, frantically looking for Mitchell. It must take somewhere between twenty seconds and infinity before it hits me that he's on the road brushing himself off

141

and staring up at the Partridge Island sky. He doesn't appear to be hurt, somehow, up and walking around just as I am with only some cuts and scrapes.

"Mitchell!" I scream his name as loudly as I can but much to my dismay, nothing happens. He doesn't even so much as flinch, just surveying the scene and watching Dean scramble around in his state of shock. Throwing myself across the divide between us, I pummel my fists into his chest over and over again, but there's no point of impact and no feeling. I can't touch Mitchell anymore. He doesn't know I'm there.

Everything human has been pulled away from me except my own consciousness. It seems to want to stay but all I want to do at that moment is curl up on the road and die.

"Paisley?" He murmurs my name, and it appears like a hazy speech bubble. At first, I don't believe that he's said it, but then a moment later he's yelling for me and sprinting toward the Escape. "Paisley!"

I run after Mitchell, my arms outstretched, feet hammering against the blacktop.

"Mitchell! I'm here. I'm right here," I cry, tears running down my cheeks in thick, wet lines. "Oh God, I thought I was dead. But you can see me, can't you? Dean couldn't hear me over the rain—"

Just at the moment where I would have been able to touch him, my fuzzy grey form slips through his body, appearing on the other side as if I've walked directly through him. I come out on the other side next to the passenger's side of the Escape, and it only takes another half a second for me to realize that I'm the unknown shape in the seat, crushed beyond recognition.

I'm dead.

Collapsing to the wet pavement, I scream at the top of my lungs and watch Mitchell throw himself toward what used to be me. I can't tell him I'm not in there anymore, but I'm sure in some way, he already knows that because instead of yanking my body from the wreckage, he takes a phone from Dean's hands and starts to dial.

I cry and yell and smash my hands on the pavement until they would ordinarily be bloody, but this time all that happens is I slowly start to float away. There's nothing for me to hold on to anymore.

TWENTY

~ MITCHELL ~

Over the sound of Georgia's arm breaking, Paisley's body caves in on itself.

There's absolutely nothing I can compare the noise to; somewhere between cracking open a thousand old books and dropping a pot of wet noodles off the roof of a two story house. It reminds me that the human body is soft inside, softer than we often give it credit for being, with emotions and organs and puncturable tissues. We often just see it as an attractive and hard exterior; skin that protects and holds things together. It's a dichotomy of nature that is easily destroyed by a metal capsule going seventy kilometers an hour.

As my own pliable and broken-down body is being torn through the Partridge Island sky, it hits me that Paisley's spot in the passenger's seat doesn't stand a chance. I call out to her, the interjection of her name muted by Paisley's startled screaming before I slam into the shoulder of the street and roll. The pebbles tear at my clothes, blasting holes in my bare legs until I finally come to a stop.

Thunder rolls in the leftover silence. There might be lightning too, but I'm facing the ground with my eyes shut so I can't tell. The soundtrack plays over and over again in my mind, rain pattering on my ripped shirt from a patch of long grass to the side of the parkway. I've been thrown clear of the Escape, the driver's side door entirely ripped from the vehicle, and at some point, the velocity of it all tossed me several meters away to land among the damp ground and wildflowers.

I roll over slowly to check and see if I'm still alive. The air smells like acrid smoke and dead blood; burning rubber still has a hot scent on the wet blacktop. My arm hurts where I've landed on it, and my legs feel as if they're on fire, but nothing appears to be broken. On the other hand, nothing appears to be working either. I've felt the feeling before: shock.

There's no speculating on how long I spend there, staring up at the sky and watching the heavy droplets fall from above, hit me in the eyes, and roll off my skin. It could be ten seconds, ten minutes, or ten hours until it becomes obvious that nothing else on the parkway is moving except rivers of rain mixed with the crimson of blood. Paisley's voice has gone hoarse and faded into the black, and I've listened to her die.

That's when the panic sets in.

"Paisley!"

I yell out her name because it's the first word that my lips form, even though my aching head knows she won't respond. Flopping over in the grass, I crawl my bloody knees over the lawn toward the broken lights of the Escape before grappling to my feet and running. The passenger's side is smashed in halfway to the back seat and a dazed figure stands in the middle of the double yellow line, ripping frantically at the metal.

I fall just as Dean's outline crosses my line of vision.

"G! Just a little bit farther—I'll call for help. I'm not hurt, at least not enough."

A shadow of a cell phone flicks out what's left of the window with a pained groan, and the shaky body reaches for it on the pavement, eyes locking on me.

"Mitchell? Shit—Mitchell, are you okay?" His hair sticks all over his face as he crouches down next to me.

"I'm alive." I cough, holding my hand out in a blissful moment of clarity. "But I'm no good for getting anyone out of those cars. Give me G's phone, and I'll call for help while you clear everyone out. I mean, you're good, right?"

"I'm good enough." He hands the phone over, and the bright light of the device explodes through the shattered screen. I can't see much of anything through the cracks, so with my one good eye I punch in 911 and wait for the line to ring. The rain comes down in sheets, pollution from the air and the clouds and the atmosphere is stinging the cuts on my skin.

Ring.

Dean helps Georgia climb through the window, her right arm mangled and her face bloody in the moonlight.

Ring.

Georgia collapses next to me on the grass as Dean rushes to Taryn's side of the Escape. He seems to know somewhere deep down that there's nothing for him to do that will help Paisley or the driver of the other car.

Ring.

"9-1-1, what's your emergency?"

A thousand thoughts roll through my head, metaphorical questions that could offer an insight into what exactly my crisis is coming to. I'd be eternally grateful if there were a way to roll it all up into a succinct little ball so the woman on the phone can understand the magnitude of what is going on. I wish she knew about the cancer and the drinking and how I professed my love for Paisley only to have it destroyed by the weather on this island.

And the wedding. We were going to get married.

"Hello? 9-1-1. Please state your emergency. If you are unable to speak, please tap the receiver against a hard surface."

"Hi—my friends and I were just hit head-on by another vehicle. We're on the highway to Gulf Bridge."

I'm surprised at my clarity.

"And what's your name?"

"Mitchell Anders." My voice says the familiar name, but none of it feels like my own.

"Okay, Mitchell. I've dispatched crews to come down your way. Can you see any signs so I can relay how far to send them?"

I try my hardest to think about what was going on outside of the Escape. I was so focused on Paisley and the rain everything else going on in the real world seemed cloudy. Then I remember a big green highway sign, maybe a kilometer back, with exit 8A in bold lettering.

"There was a sign a little while ago for Julietteville. It said the exit was coming up soon."

"Okay. That's good—we have police nearby. Thank you." There's some typing in the background. "Now, can you tell me if there are any injuries? What do you see?"

There's carnal wreckage. There are people dying. There are smoke and ashes and twisted steel and lightning. Out of the corner of my eye, there is Georgia's pale face and awkward arm and bloodied everything but none of that helps. That's not what she's asking, and that's not why the woman on the phone is trying to keep me talking.

"The front passenger's side of my car is entirely smashed in. My friend is sitting here, and her arm is definitely broken. One of the others is trying to get a girl out of the back seat. The other driver was on the wrong side of the road."

"Are the lights on the vehicles working? If someone else drove down the highway would they be able to see you?"

"Yes."

I listen to more typing as Dean wiggles Taryn from the Escape, her body floppy against his embrace. Her leg is caught between the wreckage, crushed and keeping her from being unbound. Dean recognizes it too.

"Mitchell! I need help! Can you give the phone to Georgia?"

I glance over to my left, Georgia staring off into the distance as if nobody is even around. Her arm is held close to her chest, the broken bone apparent in the way it is resting. It looks painful, more painful than my scrapes and the throbbing in my head, but Georgia isn't screaming. She isn't crying. She's just nothing. Empty.

"G—can you talk to the lady on the phone?" I'm almost like a mother consoling a shocked child. "You just need to answer her questions. Someone is coming to help."

There's a barely perceptible nod, but I take it as affirmation and shove the cell phone into her bloodied hand. She speaks, but as soon as I'm free of the device I'm already running to Dean, Taryn propped against his shoulders. Paisley's shirt pokes through the wreckage in the front seat, but most of her body is hidden by glass and steel. She isn't moving. I didn't expect that she would be, but I still can't entirely process that we aren't going to be able to save her. She's just next, is all.

"Her leg is caught," Dean directs me, gesturing vaguely. "See if you can crawl around and free it. I'm afraid if she stays with it like this too long she might end up losing it. I don't want to just pull her and rip her apart."

I don't ask him how in the hell he came up with that theory. I do as I'm told, crawling under Taryn to prop myself against broken glass and decimated metal. Her leg is squashed between the front passenger seat and the displaced middle console. The only way I might be able to get her out is to use what little strength I have to kick forward the front seat, or peel away the fragmented plastic from her skin. I try the former, but nothing budges, so I'm stuck with the latter.

Piece after bleeding piece punctures Taryn's leg, and soon my fingers are soaked in red. I can't tell what if it belongs to who anymore but I keep tearing at the plastic, edging her leg to one side, until, to the best of my knowledge, she's free.

"What do you see?" Dean shrugs Taryn against his body as I lean between unidentified parts and check on my handiwork.

"She should be good now. Her leg was kind of impaled."

The word makes me want to throw up. The thick crimson

liquid all over my arms makes me want to get sick as well, but I don't. I need to help Paisley. She's been so patient and quiet, and even though that means something, my brain refuses to accept that it defines anything.

With a bit of a struggle, Dean hoists Taryn the rest of the way out of the vehicle and half-drags her along the pavement to rest by Georgia. He's using Georgia's cardigan to stop the blood coming from Taryn's wound. Instead, I reach forward and unbuckle Paisley's seat belt so Dean will be able to pull her free. Because once she's free, she will be just like the rest of us—a little messed up but alive.

Twirling lights and sirens start to approach, and as the seat belt button finally clicks to release, I make the mistake of looking up instead of getting the hell out of that goddamn SUV.

Paisley is dead.

It hits me like a whole other vehicle, right in the heart.

Paisley is *dead*.

The whole front of the car has crashed into her chest, glass-patterned shatters of bone and skin. Her face is a mess of pats of blood and car fragments, blood dripping down the side of her head where her eyes stare, blankly, into the abyss of the night. I count from ten back to one before I puke all over the inside of the Escape, and then suddenly I'm hysterical, and Dean is removing me from the back seat as the police rush to surround us. Soon behind them is the rest of the first responders; fire, emergency medical services. They work as if we're a series of logical steps, a checklist of barricades and stretchers and shock and verification. They wrap us in blankets and take Taryn first, one man doing CPR on her chest, then another takes Georgia. The world is full of lights and flashes and blood as I watch two men pull the passenger's side of the Escape apart only to have Paisley's corpse fall on the pavement.

Then I start screaming—a ghostly moan of tears—like I'm haunted by the image of Paisley's wrecked body. Once I collapse against the edge of one of the ambulances, Dean finds me and wraps his allotted soft grey blanket around me, hiding my battered face from the wreckage of the world. I want to punch fate in whatever vulnerable body part it has and replace Paisley's death with my own. Instead, I'm curled up like a scared little songbird, that goddamn song from the radio still playing until a man in uniform cuts a wire.

Then the world goes dead. Like Paisley did. Like I will too, someday.

A woman in uniform talks to me but I don't make any sense. Dean must explain something to her because then there's a little pinch on my arm and my heart seems to stop beating. The feeling is only temporary, but my body cries for it to be permanent. My eyes glaze over, and I'm shifted onto a flat surface, a white sheet placed over my shivering body.

The hospital is antiseptic and familiar, despite the different location.

Island General Hospital has that same atmosphere as all hospitals do; matching white lights that buzz along long ceilings, stark curtains and blanched bedsheets waiting to house the next victim. It's all bright and cheery and plain and morbid, meant to be easily bleached and washed for the next person to bleed on through the doors. On top of that, the structure of the hallways is always twisting and turning, with colored dots on the floor and matching signs to direct visitors where to go. A funny thought crosses my mind, contemplating if the doctors who work here ever get lost in this place, following little, shaded breadcrumbs.

We were told we would follow the blue dots. I would have thought the dots in an ER would be red. Red seems more urgent than blue, but maybe that's part of the point.

Dean and I sit huddled in the waiting room, two shaking bodies on worn out chairs with nowhere else to go. A television flickers back and forth on some news bulletin for Vancouver, almost an entire country away and still making it to a tiny island's local station. The both of us are staring at it as if we're witnessing the most interesting event in the world, as opposed to being a couple of people who just had their friend die in front of their eyes. There's something about the silence and the distraction that makes it all go away.

"Do you think we ought to call home?" Dean leans back in his seat and stretches his legs. "Or do you reckon someone's already called our parents? Georgia's dad, maybe?"

I shrug. "I don't know. I don't even know what I would tell them. That there's been an accident, I guess. I don't even know what happened. It hasn't hit me yet. Not really."

Dean crumples back on to himself under the charcoal-colored wool, and an almost perfect set of fingerprints dots the hem of my shorts, probably from when I picked the plastic shards out of Taryn's skin.

"But it's not like you forget, right? I mean, you know that Pais—"

"Yes," I hiss, choking out a lump I didn't even know was there. "I saw it. Just my brain doesn't believe it yet."

I don't mean to sound as angry as the words come out, but my reaction seems to shut Dean up and put his focus back on the television. The screen switches over to show some hurricane in Asia, monsoon rains demolishing little villages of huts in one fell swoop. I'm about ninety percent of the way to a panic attack, and it's all I can do to block out the sounds of the gurney wheels in the background, whooping ambulance sirens looping outside. Leaning my head again the back of the chair, I have to close my eyes and pretend those flood waters are going to pick me up and carry me away.

We must sit like that for three-quarters of an hour, watching nothing and trying to breathe. After that, Doctor Hart pushes through the double doors to the emergency wing, beckoning to the two of us.

"Dean, Mitchell? Come on."

I lift my head at the sound of his familiar voice, the one that used to call Georgia home for dinner or telephone my parents if we were regularly misbehaving. Dean unravels himself from his blanket while I tuck mine closer around me, feeling a strong sense of attachment and security to the slab of fabric. Something about it helps me hold everything in and also keeps me safe from everything I could be feeling on the outside.

A man with a cane watches us traipse along the cold tile floor, pushing our way through the doors. At that moment something strange occurs to me: there aren't any clocks on the walls to tell me what time it is or count how many hours have passed since our lives changed. The only thing I assume is that the world keeps moving forward even though my mind remains implanted in the past.

We head straight down the hall, take our first left, then Doctor Hart pulls back a curtain for partition number seven.

"I've found you some visitors, Georgia Peach."

Georgia is propped sitting up in the bed, a heavy and clean white cast on her arm. She's been cleaned up, but some of her cuts and bruises remain visible, particularly those that have inflated as lumps on her face. Dean tried to play it cool in front of Doctor Hart, I can tell, and he's doing a good job at it until Georgia wipes at her watery eyes with her functional hand. At that point, it's clear that they feel something more for each other than what they've been letting in. It isn't all casual and low-key—there's something serious and adult about what they mean to each other.

It's nice. I'm glad for them, in a way.

Doctor Hart turns his head as Dean plants a kiss of Georgia's swollen lips, as much privacy as one can give in such close quarters.

"Hi, Mitchell. You look cozy." Her telltale quirky smile is plastered back on her face, presumably a side effect of some of the painkillers. "Give me one of those grey blankets, I want it for my bed at home. The grey will match my accent wall."

She sniffs back another wave of tears as I take a seat on the crumpled white sheets at the end of her bed. Dean finds his way to an old and flowery chair, while Doctor Hart meddles around with the medical equipment.

"So, Georgia," he begins. "Doctor Brossard says you've broken your ulna. You've got some nerve compression so there might be continued numbness until you heal up. The break is moderately bad, but we think you don't need pins. I'm going to go get some more information on Taryn from the nurse at the desk."

Doctor Hart brushes past the curtain and pulls it shut. Once he's gone, Georgia loses her dopey smile.

"Guys, I can't feel goddamn anything. I'm numb up to my ears. I worried all the way here I was going to be a paraplegic, but the guy in the ambulance said I was just going through emotional trauma. Are you guys okay?" Georgia looks back and forth between Dean and me.

She giggles, and it becomes obvious how doped up she is; if she remembers what happened in the same way Dean and I do.

I nod. "We're fine. Scrapes mostly. Dean has whiplash according to the paramedics."

"Yeah, my neck feels weird." He shrugs, then winces a little.

"I'm going to be able to go home in another little bit. Well, back to the hotel with Dad. He's leaving the conference early tomorrow. Have you heard anything about Paisley or the driver of the other car?" Georgia asks the question so innocently it's as if she's had an entire mental block of the actual accident.

Just then, Doctor Hart pokes his head around the partition.

"Taryn's up on floor six. They've stabilized her and said we can visit. By we, I mean Dean and Mitchell. You're not going anywhere for another hour or so, Peach."

"What about Paisley?" She asks, a lump catching in my throat as his name forms on her lips. "I mean, she's—"

Dean places his hand on her arm, and she shuts up, her father stepping back into the sanctuary of our tiny room.

"They permitted me to verify her body," he says in a low and private voice. "But her parents are on their way to confirm and make arrangements. They didn't want to talk much over the phone."

"Wait," Georgia seems to resurrect in a moment of clarity. "Paisley, did she—?"

The wheels turning in her head grind on my soul.

She doesn't know, but she's starting to find out.

I can't take this room anymore. It's suffocating me with its pallid paint and stagnant smell, and every split second Paisley's name hangs in the air like a dying heartbeat, my chest is going to explode. Pushing past the curtain of Georgia's bed, I hug the stupid grey blanket emergency around myself and half run back down the hallway and out the double doors into the bright lights of the waiting room. The man from earlier isn't in his chair anymore, the triage desk is empty, and the only person in one of the blue fabric chairs is a young woman with a baby who has the same bright eyes as Paisley.

That does me in.

I collapse on the floor, dry heaving over and over and over again, the tears and the emotions making me dizzy. Nobody seems to notice that I'm there on the floor falling apart, or maybe they do, and they know the exact feeling of anguish I'm experiencing. Coughing and crying until I can't breathe any longer I crawl through the front doors of Island General Hospital and throw myself into the leftover sprinkles of rain. They mix with the tears on my face until I can't tell where my feelings end and the weather starts. Time goes on, even in the absence of clocks. I have nowhere to go, nowhere to be, and so I sit on the curb and wait for life to end.

Instead, Doctor Hart shows up.

By the time he does, I'm soaked again, sitting with my feet in the gutter, screaming Paisley's name and cursing God for not taking me.

TWENTY-ONE

~ MITCHELL ~

The morning is sunny, without a cloud in the sky except for one tiny blip I pretend is Paisley's soul. It would have been the perfect day for us to get married, a little elopement on Partridge Island. I picture us standing on the Gulf Shore together, Paisley in an ivory lace dress, one we bought from a local maritime shop, and me in my plaid dress shirt that was stored away in the bottom of my duffel bag. We'd be smiling as waves washed over the edge of the beach, and I'd be holding her hand amidst the salty breeze.

Instead, I'm still at Island General, sitting at a picnic table out on the grass and waiting for Georgia to be sent home.

I'm not a religious or a spiritual person by any means, but the puffy little spot of white hanging over the top of the hospital acts as an artificial halo. It's kind of a comforting thought, thinking of her up in the deep blue yonder, looking down on us and hopefully saying that every little thing's going to be all right.

The sliding doors open, and Dean is pushing Georgia in a wheelchair with her father walking behind, a backpack hanging from one hand and a laptop bag crossed over his chest.

"Mitchell? You ready to head home? I called your mother a few minutes ago and let her know we'd be on our way shortly."

The question hangs in the air for a moment before I respond. I don't feel ready to leave this Island because it's as if I'm leaving a part of myself behind on it. Unfortunately for me, nobody else knows why. I mean, they do, in the sense that they know something was happening between Paisley and me, but they don't know about the wedding, the proposal, or anything else of the sort.

I guess when I think about it deeply enough, there was no wedding. We had no plans; I just wanted to buy that girl a ring and make her the happiest person alive while she still was just that —alive.

"Yeah," I respond, my voice low and mumbled. "I'm ready."

As I close myself into Georgia's family Suburban, I give a little nod to that cloud way up there; an homage to Paisley that she may rest in peace—or haunt the shores. Whichever strikes her best.

The drive across Gulf Bridge back to Hollyberry Subdivision takes another two hours, every ten seconds of which I flinch due to passing cars. Georgia's father clearly starts to notice my anxiety about a quarter of the way through the trip, letting me know there's a bottle of Ativan in the center console if I could use it. I contemplate the idea, but drugging my fear isn't about to make it go away, though it may make it more manageable at the moment.

When I get home, I'm a ball of nerves, and my mother has an absolute fit. I don't think I've been hugged so much in my life as I am in the ten minutes following my arrival. The last thing I want to do is talk about the accident, relay any information about our trip, or list of the injuries of everyone else, so I immediately excuse myself to my room and shut the door. Nobody bothers me, not even for dinner. I guess they must think I'm just processing this whole thing. Maybe I am, and maybe I'm ignoring it.

I stay in there for three days, except for running one tiny errand, until I finally get a text message from Georgia asking if I'm going to the funeral.

Georgia: *It's today, you know.*

I didn't know. I haven't left my room for days, but I don't tell her that.

Mitchell: *What time again?*

Georgia: *Eleven. Dean and I thought maybe we'd go to lunch afterward.*

The last thing I want to do is get dressed and socialize, but I tell Georgia I'll consider it.

Georgia: *Why don't you get ready and come over? We can all go together. Dean'll drive us.*

Mitchell: *Okay.*

I shuffle myself underneath my blankets, kicking them off of my legs just as there's a knock at my door. The pattern is unfamiliar, so it isn't my mother.

"Yeah?"

The knob turns, and Nolan appears in the threshold.

"Hey." He looks older, somehow, standing there staring at me, watching me fall apart at the idea of crawling out of bed. "You going to come today?"

"When did you get home?" My voice croaks from lack of use, and I run my hand through my hair, separating all the stuck-together bits. "And yeah, I was just texting Georgia. I'm going to go with her and Dean."

"Good, you need to leave this room. It smells in here."

I snort, the most noise I've made since leaving the hospital. Nolan grins, standing there in his tartan pajama pants, satisfied that he's made a tiny breakthrough in getting me to exist back in the real world.

"Fine."

"Mom's making bacon downstairs if you want some. You should probably eat."

"What's with all of this paternal instinct? Shouldn't you be up here telling me to get over myself?"

Nolan sighs. "I know what it's like to love a girl, Mitchell. I'm not a complete asshole. Now get up, take a shower, and eat some breakfast before you go over to Georgia's. Otherwise, you're just going to scare everyone."

With that, he closes the door before I get a chance to respond.

An hour later, I'm sitting in Georgia's room with Dean and a cigarette, staring at Taryn's empty window. It's almost like I've been asleep until this very moment, transfixed in my mind or hypnotized, and only something in this second has broken the spell to remind me that there's a great big world outside my head. Smoke coils from my mouth and trickles in the thick summer sun like grey ribbons, misting into the leaves of the oak tree that meets between the two properties.

Cracking my neck from side to side, I try to loosen up the tension that's been sitting in my vertebrae since the accident. The effort is entirely in vain, although something about the repetitive nature of the action soothes me. I guess maybe I think it's doing something when it isn't helping at all. There's a word for that —placebo.

I crush the end of my cigarette against the bottom of the new ashtray Georgia bought at one of the Island shops. The little red end of the stick smolders.

"What are you thinking about?"

Her voice comes from behind me, and I turn.

Georgia is reclined on her bed, hair splayed out across a pile of pillows, and her arms are resting up over her head, while Dean is strumming some random chords on a periwinkle blue guitar made for a kid. Her cast has been doodled on in a rainbow of colors, mostly by Dean who has taken to leaving little artistic cartoons and carefully selected song lyrics on the white plaster. There are also hearts casually scattered around, some big and some so tiny it's hard to pick them out. Since the accident, they've moved their relationship into a new level; one where they say the things that they want to get out in case they happen to run out of time as Paisley and I did.

"Nothing," I reply immediately, leaning back against the

window frame. "Just wondering when Taryn's going to come back home. I'm surprised they didn't transfer her."

"They did," Georgia corrects, pushing herself upright on the mattress. She's clad in a little black dress that rumples around her bare knees, a stark difference from the kaleidoscope of patterns and shades that are present in her room. A grey blanket—Dean's grey blanket from the accident—is at the foot of the bed. I don't know why she wanted to keep it after all that happened, but her father told me that sometimes people have their distinct way of grieving. Maybe it's her way of holding on to Paisley.

I brush a speckle of ash from my coal-colored pants.

"Oh right, today. They're sending her to Birch Valley today. Wouldn't it be weird if she ended up in the same room as Paisley was in?"

"Cancer's floor two." She swings her legs off the side of the bed and sighs, itching at the hem of her cast.

"Guess it won't happen then."

Dean doesn't say anything; he hums along to a song he's writing in his head and strums at the strings absently. There's a rift of silence between us all, a gap that's been growing since we hit the turnoff for Birch Valley. We've been trying to act like everything's normal, like Paisley isn't dead and Taryn isn't still in the hospital, and our trip ended up being the grand finale in our best friend's life.

My phone interrupts the vast space of nothing as it rings a pitiful little alarm, salvaged somehow in perfect condition from the crash.

"Time to go. Mom and Nolan are already there." The words come out of my mouth with a stifled cough, the leftover tobacco and marijuana burning my lungs. I've admittedly been smoking a lot more since we've returned, and Robbie Marks has been more than happy to supply my habit to fund his car expense account.

"All right then." Georgia picks herself up off the bed, adjusting her outfit with one good hand.

This tension is misery, and Dean finally addresses it.

"What's wrong with us?"

Georgia twists her eyebrows together as if she's trying to curl them into a pretzel, and sighs.

"Do you really want to do this now? Before Paisley's funeral?"

It's a loaded question, but I can't tell who is holding the gun.

"No."

I cross the floor of the bedroom, my black dress socks scuffing against the sky blue rug, and I close Georgia's bedroom door, leaving her and Dean behind. Muffled voices come through the wood, and they're definitely talking about me because the words only make sense in that singular context. I slide my back along the wall and listen at the door because there are things to be said and words to be heard that couldn't be expressed in front of my face.

"What the hell do you think is wrong with us, Dean? Why would you say anything in front of Mitchell? Can't you tell he's about a half a second away from falling apart?" Georgia's voice has a distinct tone of annoyance.

"We knew she was going to die, Georgia! Just because it happened in a way that nobody expected doesn't make it any less real."

Dean has a valid point, but it's still a painful one, and my eyes start to water. The sensation is nothing short of annoying.

"It's not just about the accident, you ass. It's about everything else. Think about what he saw. Think about what he did."

"What about what I saw and what I did? I pulled people out of those cars. I dragged you out through a window for Christ's sake. I tried to save the driver of the other vehicle by doing CPR until the ambulance got there." Dean's voice turns into a hiss at the end.

"Please. I'm not discounting you. But right now this isn't about you. I'll always be here and thankful for what you did. You're so strong—stronger than any of us. But don't let that change you. Don't let that make you angry. We're all going to need help to get through this one."

There's silence then, and I fill in the blanks as to what's happening until the door opens.

"Mitchell? Everything okay?" Georgia peers down at me from my spot on the floor, my face probably a heavy red from holding in my emotions.

"We were going to get married," I mumble.

"I'm sorry, what?" Dean stammers. "Did you say you were going to get married? To Paisley?"

I stare down at the floorboards.

"Mitchell, are you serious?" Georgia kneels down in front of me, placing her hands on my bent knees. "You asked her to marry you? When did this even happen?"

"Right before everything went downhill. She said yes. I had it all planned out in my head. This wasn't exactly a part of the plan."

"Oh God," Georgia breathes. "I'm so sorry. I didn't know...I mean, I had no idea that you guys had even—"

Dean sets a hand on Georgia's shoulder as she stands up and starts to cry into his chest. I can't look at her, or him for that matter, instead of sidling up against the wall and leaving them alone once again, standing in the hallway and trying to comfort each other in my misery.

TWENTY-TWO

~ MITCHELL ~

There is a vase filled with white roses next to a plain redwood urn, and a picture of Paisley behind it all. The photograph hits me especially hard; I remember taking it in the fall just before school started, around the time the leaves began to change just a little bit around the edges. Paisley is sitting on the edge of her roof with a guitar in her hands, strumming something awful because she had no idea how to play. In a picture, you can't tell, and instead, she looks deep in thought as if she's playing the melody of an old country song about love or death or moving on.

Dean and Georgia have given me some space, taking equal amounts for themselves to the point that I don't know where they even are in the room anymore. Standing here on my own, I stare at the little chest that holds what's left of Paisley's body, all reduced to ash and held within the tiny walls. It's amazing to me that something so big can be reduced to something so small, a little pile of bits like one of our cigarettes. I'm more than well aware that scientifically we're made up of mostly water, but it's hard to picture exactly how much of our bodies are liquid until we're able to observe the leftovers.

An uncomfortable crawling starts in the dredges of my stomach, a rumbling as if I'm hungry but with more intensity, making my eyes tear up. I can't tell if it's a sensation caused by the pain medication the emergency room doctor prescribed me, or if I'm finally falling apart. Maybe it's because I'm looking at the inevitable end of life. A tiny box on a table, with mourning people milling around trying to figure out why life has to be so awful sometimes.

I glance at the people gathered in the small church, some sitting in the pews with their heads bowed, others walking around and whispering to one another in hushed voices that carry farther than they normally would. The whole place is an echo chamber, and I swear the tears of Paisley's family resonate off the walls. Even my brother Nolan has bleary eyes when he walks up to me, and I don't think I've ever seen him show any emotion before. Then again, growing up, he was always the stronger of the two Anders boys.

"Hi, Mitch. You doing all right? Mom says you can come to sit with us if you want. We're saving spots for Georgia and Dean as well, wherever they've gone off to."

"Thanks," I stammer, trying to regain my composure. I'm dizzy again, but I'm always dizzy now. "I should probably just sit down. I kind of don't know what to do with myself."

I follow Nolan down the aisle way to an empty seat in the front row. Nearly the whole aisle is vacant, the Watts family greeting guests by the main doors and receiving condolences.

"So," Nolan clears his throat. "Too bad about Taryn. Mom says she's being transferred today."

"Yeah." I fiddle with the edge of my black shirt as I adjust my position in the hard seat. "Hopefully she'll be okay in a few more days. Joffre said her hearing is coming back a little, but the doctors still expect she'll have lost most of it."

"Taryn's always been strong. I'm sure she'll find a way to cope."

I nod, scratching my face, itchy because I hadn't bothered to shave since before we came home from Partridge Island. Silence stands between my brother and me, and an understanding falls over me at the moment: we aren't kids anymore. No more wrestling on the rec room floor, getting bruises from falling out of trees. Now we're just trying to wrangle ourselves around real life and not get hurt by all of the things that inevitably don't end up killing us.

"Listen, Mitchell. I'm not stupid. It's clear that something was going on between you two. You don't have to hide it. She was always a special part of your life."

I bristle at the loaded question, but a smile creeps across my face and gives me away. Was there something going on? Absolutely. But who has to know exactly how much?

I shrug. "Kind of. We didn't have much time."

Nolan nods as if he knows more than he's letting on.

"Paisley never did care about time. She's so patient—was patient. Not like me. I can't wait for anything."

I stifle a little laugh, as Georgia and Dean appear behind me, squashing themselves into the end of the row. Georgia's face is flushed and red, and Dean has the allure of a fresh smoke and pine tree air freshener. He looks like he's in the wrong era as always—a Gatsby hat on his head polishing off his 1920s apparel. He and Georgia together are a mishmash of beautiful styles across the ages, complete with the expressions of two people in a complicated scenario. Maybe the accident has changed them, to a degree, and I don't know what it will mean once Georgia goes away for college halfway across the country.

"Hey," Georgia murmurs, sitting down next to me and smoothing the skirt of her black dress with her casted arm. Dean gives me a curt nod, the gesture meant for Nolan as well.

"Didn't think we'd ever be here. At least, not this soon. It seems, wrong, you know."

"I know."

A little bell chimes, indicating the start of the service.

The sea of people moves from the front of the church to take seats, parents gathering with groups of family members and class-mates to fill the tiny atrium. It only takes a minute for everyone to find a place, the shuffle of feet and feelings stirring up the stagnant air of the old building. It takes a minute for Old Pastor James to populate his spot on the altar, and a sobbing hush falls over the congregation. He moves slowly to stand in front of us, his ambulation creaky with age. From what I recall, he's been in this town longer than it has existed, back when the Sawyer River was named after that kid who jumped in trying to save his sister.

"Hello, everyone," he begins, wringing his wrinkled hands. "It is with great sorrow that we are gathered here today to honor the life of Paisley Anne Watts. And although we have these feelings of sadness, loss, and bereavement, it is important that we remember how Paisley lit up our lives and contributed to our happiness."

He clasps his fingers together in front of him, almost in prayer but not quite, as if he still has more to say.

"Please Lord, take Paisley into your embrace and grant us the peace of knowing she is with you."

There's a rumble in the crowd like a wave—amen, amen, amen.

"Now as I understand, we will first have a few words by Paisley's friend, Mitchell."

Everyone turns to look at me, and for a moment, I panic; I didn't anticipate having to speak, and I definitely don't have anything prepared. Thankfully the anxiety only lasts a second as Nolan drops a piece of paper into my lap.

"I didn't want to give you too much notice because I knew you'd freak out, but I told Mrs. Watts that you'd say something personal. I took the liberty of writing the speech myself because I figured whatever you were going to say would be mushed up crap. Just read it."

"Nolan, I—"

"Trust me, kid brother. Just read it, and you'll be fine."

Every other time Nolan has told me to trust him, it's ended in catastrophe, but I have to hope that he at least has the common decency not to pull a stunt at a funeral. Mom gives me a little smile as I stand, a tissue grasped in her right hand, and I hold the paper in front of me with both hands as my dress shoes make audible taps on the tile floor. Tears start to form in my eyes, and as soon as I reach the top step of the podium and bend up the microphone, I'm biting my own lip to keep myself from losing composure.

Nolan's perfect writing is clear on the white sheet, and the letters are big enough for me to see even though my eyes are quickly filling up with tears. The paper simply says 'tell the truth.'

"Hi everyone." My voice projects through the congregation, a little shaky but stronger than I expected it to sound. "I was just saying to Georgia and Dean that we're here a little earlier than expected. I thought I'd have more time to put together the words I wanted to say to Paisley, but unfortunately, time doesn't always work out at you want it to. Thankfully, I have a brother who understands feelings better than I do so that you can thank him for the words I'll say in a moment since he gave me a little cheat sheet. In case you can't read it way at the back, all it says is 'tell the truth.'"

A tiny rumble of laughter escapes the crowd as I hold up the crumpled piece of paper. I swipe my gaze up and down the aisles at the sea of black and navy blue, women and men with tissues to their faces and the backs of their hands wiping at their eyes, and I have to tell them all that Paisley and I were more than just friends. I loved her.

"As many of you know, Georgia was good enough to organize a little last minute vacation for Paisley to try and get her bucket list completed. I'm happy to say we got a lot of things done: getting Paisley a tattoo, having a bonfire, going on the last trip as best friends. However, what most of you don't know is that one thing on Paisley's list was to fall in love, and get married."

I pause, for effect and my voice cracks as a result.

"The night before Paisley passed, I asked her to marry me, and she said yes. Paisley, if we would have had more time, would have been my wife. That trip helped us realize that we were in love, absolutely."

Casting my eyes over the front row there's Paisley's mom sobbing into Roger's shoulder, my mother being handed a packet of tissues from Nolan, and Dean and Georgia holding hands and not letting go.

"Of course, when I asked her to marry me I wasn't exactly prepared. I didn't have a ring, and I hadn't thought about how expensive they are. So instead, we decided that we'd get matching tattoos. Of course, since she had already just gotten one, we planned on going back to the artist at the Boardwalk the next day and for me to get the same one as well. Even though we didn't end up having real vows, her word was enough. I went and got my tattoo anyway."

I push up the sleeve of my suit jacket to expose a still-red mirror image of Paisley's forget-me-not tattoo, holding my wrist up for the crowd to see.

"She was my best friend, and I'll never forget her."

There is silence, and I step down from the podium to a sound-track of tears. I'm sure she won't forget me either. And someday we will be together again.

TWENTY-THREE

~ PAISLEY / MITCHELL ~

Months roll by as if nothing happened, and our lives weren't monumentally changed by what occurred that summer.

September was a blur of moving parts: Dean enrolled into his welding course at Sawyer College, Georgia flew off to Ontario to pursue her nursing degree, and Taryn moved one city over where she met up with that girl she was texting from the photo-sharing app. I was the only one who seemed to feel lost still. I dropped my scholarship to New York State that I received last minute, picked up a job stuffing envelopes at a marketing firm down on Main, and ended up with a prescription for antidepressants that I only took half the time. When I consumed medication, it made me feel weird, like I was trying to forget about Paisley and the way she made me feel in all the time we had together.

Once October and autumn melt into Birch Valley, I start to think maybe for Thanksgiving we could all have a little reunion—a coming home to Hollyberry celebration where we tell each other lies about how much we've grown up and how we aren't still totally devastated. A text goes out from me to Dean, Taryn, and Georgia; Dean replies right away, Georgia a few days later, and Taryn not at all. If we didn't have cell phones, I'd blame it on her hearing loss, but from what has been passed along the gossip grapevine, she's making out perfectly well for herself. Although for all I'm aware of, she's struggling too, somewhere along the line, and just doesn't want to let anyone know that she's falling apart just as much as we are.

So now, it's the holiday evening, and I'm sitting in my bedroom with my playlist turned up ten decibels too high, waiting for Georgia and Dean to appear in my doorway. Turkey dinner is still settling in my stomach even though I didn't eat much of anything, and I've hoarded a couple of bags of chips and some bottles of Mountain Dew from the spare storage kitchen in the basement. It almost seems like we're reverting in age back to when we were children, the summer week on Partridge Island with weed and liquor only a sneaky event with no real consequence. For the sake of nostalgia, we should probably all have a couple of beers and hash out everywhere everything went wrong. The problem is that Georgia still blames herself for the accident since the trip was her idea after all.

I'm just waiting, now—waiting and thinking—while binge-reading linking Wikipedia articles when an email pops into my inbox. Usually I wouldn't even bother checking it, my messages piling up over the last number of weeks, but there's something familiar about the Hotmail address. It takes a second for it to hit me —songbird04. That's the nickname I gave to Paisley when she tried out for the choir.

Pausing the rock song coursing through my computer speakers, I click on the pop-up notification on the corner of the screen. My hand starts to shake as the browser loads, my heart expecting something that my mind hasn't quite caught up to, then a message from sender Paisley Watts appears smack dab in the middle of the monitor.

Mitchell —

Immediately her voice plays over in my head.

Happy Thanksgiving. Remember last year when you tried to teach me to play guitar on the roof while Mom cooked us a ham? That was the moment I realized that I'm in love with you.

My heart drops into my toes, remembering the exact moment she's talking about because the photograph I took of that split second appeared at her funeral only months before.

I'm setting up this message and this email account as you're sleeping next to me, trying to absorb everything we've grown into while on this incredible vacation. Even though I'm sick and falling apart, it's still so clear that our feelings for each other will outlive my own lifetime. This makes me both happy and sad because although I know I won't be forgotten, I also am entirely aware that before you get this, I'll have already left. So here I am on the one year anniversary of realizing I've fallen for the boy across the street, telling you that I'm not gone—not really.

A single tear rolls down my cheek, a little salty river streaking my skin. As I scroll down the browser window to read the next portion of the email, the blue of the healed tattoo flowers peeks from under the sleeve of my shirt. The more I scroll, the less I'm able to breathe, my lungs compressing with each passing millisecond and threatening to cut off my air supply completely.

I'm always here, whenever you look across the road at that empty bedroom window. I'm in Thanksgiving, memories of prom, high school, beach days at Sawyer Lake and the nostalgia of the day we all met in Hollyberry Subdivision. And now, as of last night, I'm a part of you in a different way—a way that nobody can take.

Someone once told me that sex is like gluing together two pieces of construction paper. Once that glue dries, you can't separate them without a little bit of the color transferring off onto the other sheet. In my head you're blue, and I'm red, and now we've got these little freckles of each other on our own personal stationery.

There's nothing that can stop the memory of that one night from flooding my thoughts and penetrating the part of my brain responsible for feeling things. The way Paisley looked in the light of the Partridge Island moon, stars dancing in her eyes and the bandage still on her wrist from the fresh forget-me-not tattoo. The daydream flows—every important instance of my life having Paisley there by my side. I stifle a hacking sob, my vision blurry, and my ribcage crushing all of my organs.

I hate being emotional.

Mitchell, please don't let your life stop because I'm gone. For anyone else, this message would sound trite and assuming, but after all this time I know your type and how you let things affect you more than they appear to. Please live a good life knowing that you helped me live mine—even without completing everything on my bucket list. I knew I'd never finish it all; I just wanted to spend some last time with you all, forgetting that I was sick. And, for awhile, I did forget about the cancer. So thank you for that too. Thanks for making me feel whole and beautiful. Now please go on and make the rest of the world whole and beautiful too.

At the end of the message, there's a little postscript, and I almost miss it through my watering eyes.

PS: I think in some way I always knew that you'd be the one that I'd marry. But now that I'm up in the stars don't let me be the only one that you give your heart to. Someone else deserves to be loved by you.

Forget me not,
Paisley

I'm breaking into a million tiny pieces; all the feelings that I've been holding come running out of my body in tears and heartbreak and wrenching pain in my stomach that I don't seem to be able to let go of.

Doubling over in front of my computer, I finally let myself go, crying until I'm unable to breathe or see. Paisley's words hit me hard, maybe from the sheer surprise of getting to read them again, but perhaps a little bit because I needed her permission to fall apart. She would want me to miss her, but I also know she would want me to let her go.

However, I can't let her go until I accept that she's gone, and at this moment, that's the realization that I'm having. She isn't coming back, and she wants me to remember that, accept it, and use the love I had for her to help someone else in whatever way I can.

She'd be yelling at me right now if she knew all the things that I'd done in my misery, but I would argue with her that I was probably never really meant to go to New York State. That I had only applied to make my mother happy, and at some point, you have to start making decisions for yourself—and that's what I'm doing now. Kind of.

Scrubbing tears off my face and from between the whiskers of my three-day beard, I hit the print button on my email and watch Paisley's words get transferred to a blank sheet of paper. The device churns and whirs as it completes the job, spitting out the page on the receiving tray after only a few moments. Picking up the paper, warm from the press, I push myself out of my desk chair and walk over to my far wall where Paisley's old mood board has been hung up on the wall. Pinned on it are pictures from over the years, little pieces of paper from inside fortune cookies, and other bits and bobs she found interesting throughout school; newspaper clippings and doodles from the edges of notebook pages. Right in the middle, I tack her email, a big white island in the middle of chaos.

With a shuddering sigh, I sit back down in front of my computer and stare at the screen, thinking.

I've been an idiot.

Flicking over back to Wikipedia, I browse the sequence of articles I've been searching for the past few days. They're all medical pieces about the way the body functions, emergency evacuation procedures, and crisis assistance, with a few poignant articles on CPR and general first aid. I've been trying to figure out what I did wrong in the accident, what steps I should take next time to make sure that everyone gets out alright—trying so hard to justify my actions for more than what they were. What I find at that moment, while waiting for Dean and Georgia, is that I would do it all over again, in a second; in a heartbeat.

Then it hits me.

This is what I want to do. I want to save people. And so, a theoretical light bulb goes off in my head.

I run a quick internet search on paramedic schools in and around the eastern coast. Within seconds at the top result of the search engine, I get a hit on a program on Partridge Island starting in January that is still accepting last-minute applications—Emergency Medical Training Centre in Rockabee, five minutes from the boardwalk where Paisley got her tattoo. Skimming over the admission requirements, I meet or exceed, all of the minimums, and I have all of the necessary prerequisites to apply, other than a one-thousand-word essay explaining why I want to be a paramedic. Clicking the 'apply now' button, a registration form appears on my screen, sitting right on the toolbar next to Paisley's email. She wrote to me to give my heart to someone else, but maybe instead of it being a person, I will throw myself into something I'm passionate about—something that might help me heal from everything that happened over the course of the summer.

It only takes a few minutes for me to get to the essay section of the application once I've filled in my contact information, and inside that blank space, I start to write about all of us, about the bucket list, the accident, and Paisley. I tell whoever is on the other end of the form that I freed Taryn from having an impaled leg, that I relayed information to the 911 operator, and that my terminally ill girlfriend was crushed to death by the impact of another vehicle. I leave out the part about that I had just asked her to marry me, only because it doesn't feel right to tell a stranger something like that. The words flow quickly, almost too fast for my fingers to catch up with my mind, and before I'm aware of it, the field is filled with text and a story that I only hope explains in proper words the reason why I need to do this.

I take a chance and don't even bother reading my application over, hitting the submit button before I change my mind.

Leaning back in my chair, I gaze out the window across the road at the empty room that used to belong to Paisley. There's nothing to see anymore—the roof is empty like Mrs. Watts probably always wished it would be, and the curtains are drawn across the glass so I can't look inside. To my amusement, for the first time it occurs to me that the fabric has little birds patterned over top of it; sparrows, maybe. Some kind of songbird.

With a deep sigh, I prop myself up in my chair and move the mouse cursor until it hovers over the reply button on Paisley's email.

Click.

Dear Paisley,

I begin, tapping carefully on the keys and considering what I'd like to tell her. Only one thing comes to mind, and so it's the first thing I write.

Don't worry about me. Everything's going to be alright.

Don't miss your next favorite book!

Join the Fire & Ice mailing list
www.fireandiceya.com/mail.html

THANK YOU FOR READING

Did you enjoy this book?

We invite you to leave a review at the website of your choice, such as Goodreads, Amazon, Barnes & Noble, etc.

DID YOU KNOW THAT LEAVING A REVIEW...

- Helps other readers find books they may enjoy.
- Gives you a chance to let your voice be heard.
- Gives authors recognition for their hard work.
- Doesn't have to be long. A sentence or two about why you liked the book will do.

ABOUT THE AUTHOR

NICOLE BEA is a short story author and novelist who primarily focuses on writing contemporary teen fiction. An avid storyteller since childhood, she has honed her skills through a variety of educational programs including management, sociology, legal studies, and cultural diversity in the workplace, most recently engaging in coursework about communication for technologists. In addition to writing for young adults, Nicole is also a technical writer for a global manufacturer of CPAP masks, machines, and other products that manage sleep-disordered breathing.

When she isn't busy updating her manuscript portfolio, Nicole can usually be found reading, horseback riding, or pursuing her new hobby of learning to cook. She and her husband share their home in Eastern Canada with a collection of multi-colored cats and a lifetime's worth of books.

www.nicolebea.com

 twitter.com/nicolebeawrites
instagram.com/nicolebeawrites

Made in the USA
Middletown, DE
20 April 2021